INDIAN SUMMER

INDIAN SUMMER

LYLE BEBENSEE

Third Eye
London   Canada
1997

Indian Summer
© Lyle Bebensee 1997

Canadian Cataloguing in Publication Data

Bebensee, Lyle
    Indian summer

ISBN 0919581-17-X

I. Title.

PS8553.E294152 1997   C813'.54   C97-932299-5
PR9199.3.B42152 1997

Published by
Third Eye Publications Inc.
31 Claarke Road
London, Ontario, Canada
N5W 5W5

Dedicated to
all the Canadian women
who lost their husbands in World War II

Contents

I

"I hear them...I hear the thundering caribou," Christine called, soon after Jana tucked her in for the night.

How many times had the old woman told her about the caribou?

The *thundering caribou*, passing close to Christine's tent in their spring and fall migrations. For three days they came. One year it took them five days to pass by the lake. "We knew we'd have meat for winter, and the children would be warm."

On the last night Christine's mind began to wander. She lay looking up at Jana with strange eyes. "The caribou are coming. I will go with the hunters!" she called. Then her eyes filled with terror, as she watched a polar bear scatter the herd and kill her father before the other hunter could put out its eyes with his spear.

Jana took her in her arms and held her until she was quiet. "Now I will go home with the hunters," Christine whispered, and her hand slipped away from Jana's.

Christine died early this morning. Jana put the pen

down. She looked again at the words she had written in her diary, then slowly closed the cover and slid the diary into the desk drawer.

Jana lifted her eyes to the window. The barren field still held the late snow which fell in the night. It clung to the pussy willows in the ditch at the side of the road, bending them almost to the ground, their half-open buds temporarily stalled on their march into spring. And the woodlot, which on the previous evening rang to the call of returning song birds, now lay still and silent.

Jana thought of the day she met Christine. The old lady had taken her into her tent on the shore of the deep lake and given her tea, and a new pair of moccasins.

Jana smiled as she recalled trying to explain love to Christine.

"Is it like the taste of frozen caribou?" Christine asked.

"No!" Jana laughed. "It's not a taste. You see, it's a way of thinking...it's in your head."

Christine looked confused. "Love in your head?" she questioned.

"There are many kinds of love," Jana explained. "It's not always in your head. When you have wonderful feelings for someone, it's really in your heart!"

Christine looked totally bewildered.

Jana tried to explain love in more practical terms. "If I came by your snow house in the winter and found you starving, I would go back to my place and get some meat for you, even if I had only enough for myself. That would be an act of love."

Christine nodded her head. "Frozen caribou," she said. She smiled and went on stitching a moccasin.

Now it was over. The words in the diary were there to tell her that life is measured in the seasons of the caribou.

Jana picked up the telephone. "I want to speak to Robert Conlon at Arcticair," she stated. "You must not be sad when I die," Christine said. "My spirit has seen many seasons of the caribou."

"Frank here," came the voice from Yellowknife.

"Bob, please. It's important," Jana said.

"He's at the mine," Frank explained. "Maybe I can raise him on the radio if he's in the air. I'll hook you up if he answers."

"It would be wrong to grieve after such happiness," Christine said.

A voice broke through the sound of an aircraft engine.

"Bob Conlon," the voice said.

"It's Christine," Jana said, haltingly. "She died early this morning. She is on her way home." For a moment there was only the sound of the engine on the phone. Then Bob came back.

"I'm sorry."

"She will be buried on the western side of the lake, where the purple saxifrage runs up toward the rock."

"I know the place. The large rock that shades the alpine roses. Where you rebuilt the sod house."

"Yes, that's it," Jana said. "Christine told me it captures the first rays of the returning sun. She chose it for that reason."

"I'll see that she's taken care of," Bob said.

Jana put the phone down gently. What would she have done without Bob? She had leaned heavily on him when she needed help. Now she would count on him again.

She brought a cup of coffee from the kitchen and sat down at the desk. If Christine were here it would be tea, she told herself. What wonderful times they had, talking over cups of tea in the summer tent by the lake. "It takes time to find one's way," the old Inuit woman said.

Jana walked to the window. A full grown female deer, partly hidden by the saplings at the edge of the woodlot, stood motionless, its nose testing something on the cold morning air.

Jana saw a caribou. Then she caught hold of herself. She had seen a deer at that spot several times. It was quite different from the caribou three hundred and fifty miles north of Yellowknife.

II

"Jana!" Her mother's voice was determined. "Jana, your father is ready. I have all your things packed. You'll have everything you need at Winthrop Academy."

"Mother, I wish I could stay here with the other Indian children."

"Jana, you are only half-Indian. You are a bright girl, and you deserve a proper education: music, literature, and the other things which contribute to a happy and productive life. I want you to have the same chance I had. You'll be a self-reliant girl, and you'll have a much better life."

Jana watched her mother's eyes, as she drew her close and kissed her. She could see some sadness. Was that sadness because she was leaving? Maybe it was partly because of the life, she, a white woman, was forced to endure on an Indian reservation.

She heard her mother complain, sometimes, about the way the Indian women treated her. One Indian woman told her father that his white wife was a stuck-up bitch. And she knew that some Indian men were unfriendly to her father, because he worked land outside the Reserve to make extra money.

Jana's father, a Delaware Indian, rented the mission farm on the Indian reservation from the Moravian Missionary Convention. The farm, lying close to the Thames River, had been cleared by the Delaware Indians the Moravian missionaries brought with them from the thirteen American Colonies to the south.

After the War of 1812, the Moravian Missionary Enterprise came to an end, and the land fell into disuse.

Jana's father resurrected the land and made it productive again.

Some Indians said Roy Hillman was greedy for working land outside the Reserve, in addition to the mission farm.

Jana knew she had better clothes than most of the other children at the mission school.

Some of the boys said she was a "little rich

bitch," and one time they threw mud at her new coat. The teacher helped her to clean it before she went home.

When she got too big for her clothes, her mother took them to the mission office for the poor children. Some parents refused to let their children wear them. They weren't below the half-whites, they said. Jana wished their parents would let the children wear her old clothes because some of the kids weren't warm enough when they walked a long way to school in the winter.

Sometimes the young lady teacher let the students sit close to the stove when they came in the morning. And then one winter morning the young lady teacher was gone. Nobody knew why she left. Some of the older children thought it had something to do with a young preacher who came to the mission a few months before.

The older lady, who came to take the young teacher's place, made them stand up and pray to God every morning before they took their books from their desks. Jana's mother didn't seem pleased when she told her about the prayers.

She heard her mother and father talking about the prayers that night when they thought she was asleep.

"I almost went out of my mind from fear when I was a young girl," her mother said. "When there was no teacher in the room, the evangelist told us we would all burn in hell for our sins if they were not forgiven. Then he made us pray to God and say we were sorry for our sins, and ask Him to save us from hell. I used to wake up at night screaming, and I was afraid to tell my mother, because I felt guilty. Finally she figured it out."

"What did your mother do?" her father asked.

"She marched right down to that school on the day when the evangelist was there. She carried one of those pincer implements they used for castrating young bulls. She held it up for the evangelist to see when she told him to never again frighten her daughter, or any of the other young children, with stories about hellfire and brimstone. She asked him if he had ever thought of becoming a member of the castrati. It would put his evangelism on a more *elevated level*, she said."

Her mother and father laughed for a long time after that.

"Jana, come now, dear. It's time to go."

III

The long ride to Winthrop Academy in her father's car seemed as though it would never end. And the open country along the highway appeared cold and unfriendly after the woodlots Jana was always close to on the Reserve.

If her class marks had not been so high, maybe the Academy would not have accepted her when her mother wrote to them. And if her father hadn't worked so hard and made extra money, her parents would not be able to pay the Academy the money they wanted for her board, and all the things they said would help her to become a refined lady.

She tried to visualize what the Academy would look like. It might have green vines growing up the walls like the big school in the picture the young lady teacher showed them one time.

Maybe it would be spring at the Academy. As Jana thought of spring, she could almost feel the sun coming through the classroom windows onto her shoulders. She let herself slip down on the seat. Soon she was unable to resist the drowsiness....

The birds were singing in the lilac tree as she walked out the lane to go to school with the Indian children. The young teacher was at the door waiting for them. She let them stay outside and skip as long as they wanted to. Then they sang songs, and the teacher sang a funny song for them. She sang one that was more sad than funny, and her eyes looked different, and she stopped singing, and said perhaps they had sung enough for that day, and they must hurry to finish their work before school closing time. Then she helped the little ones put on their coats to go home....

"Jana, wake up dear. We are here." Her mother took a brush from her purse and brushed Jana's hair back behind her ears. She cradled her face in her two hands.

"What a pretty girl I have," she remarked, and her blue eyes said she meant it. "You'll do just fine here, dear. And you'll be a fine lady. Why, my goodness, you're only twelve, and I believe you're a fine lady already." Her mother pressed her first two fingers lightly under Jana's chin and looked right into her eyes. "Your father and I both love you. Will you remember that? We both love you." Her mother smiled again.

"Dad, you love me too, don't you?"

Her father tried to talk, but he couldn't. He just nodded and let his head drop down a little.

The Academy was a large, red brick building two storeys high. There were wide steps leading up to big doors. The doors were surrounded by a tall arch reaching almost to the top of the building. And there were some fancy carvings of strange-looking heads on each side of the arch. Her mother said they were called gargoyles.

"Class. Young ladies!" There was complete silence as the head mistress put the register down. Her steady eyes swept the room from front to back, and side to side. "My name is Miss Baxter," she stated. "We are about to begin our final semester. When we have completed this term it will be summer. I know you are all looking forward to summer. But now we must think seriously about our duties and responsibilities. I know you will endeavour to put forth your best efforts in order to accomplish your goals. And while most of you are still very young..." Miss Baxter stopped abruptly. She dropped her head a little, sweeping back her greying hair with her right hand. She gave a nervous cough and pulled herself up straight.

"We all have goals. To reach them we must persevere. We must be steadfast in our pursuit of excellence. That is the policy of our school. It is our expectation of all those who are privileged to attend this institution. I know you will honour the Academy with your very best efforts."

Goals, persevere, expectation. What did it all mean? Jana wondered.

"And now I have the honour," the mistress said, a slight smile crowding the seriousness of her face, "of introducing you to a new student, a young lady from a native reservation. She is joining us for the last semester by special arrangement.

"Jana Elizabeth Hillman, will you please stand up and tell us what you hope to accomplish at this Academy." Jana felt glued to her seat. Then she broke loose and stood up. Her lips started to move, but no words would come. Some of the other girls looked as though they would burst if she didn't say something soon. She glanced at the head mistress, and saw that her stiff face had softened a little. At last some of her mother's words seemed ready to meet her trembling lips.

"I...I have come to the Academy to learn literature and music, and the other things which will help me to have an interesting life. And I want to be a fine lady." Some of the girls took deep breaths of relief and applauded politely. The head mistress stood smiling for a few seconds, then brushed her eyes across the faces of the girls.

"Splendid," she remarked. "Now, before I go, I have a special announcement to make: The mayor of Woodstock has advised me that the lieutenant governor of Ontario will be attending our gradua-tion ceremonies in June. We are all very pleased.

"It is time to get down to our studies. Miss Broome, your ballet instructor will be waiting for you." She turned back at the door. "Good Luck!"

As the students lined up to go to the audito-rium, Jana felt the sting in the eyes of some of the girls. But there were other girls who looked com-pletely friendly. Her mother had told her that was the way it would be.

III

Summer! Jana stepped out of the car. Her feet seemed to hardly touch the ground as she bounced up the path toward the house. She swung her eyes from the garden to the woodlot and back. How good it was to be home among familiar things again! She was free of the constrictions of school for a full two months, free to roam the fields and countryside with her friends again.

Things had not changed much on the reservation. The children were still happy and boisterous. Some of the younger ones seemed reluctant to approach her when they heard a difference in her speech and saw that she walked with her head held straighter. Soon the differences didn't matter, and they laughed and skipped and sang silly songs the way they had always done.

One evening that summer, Jana heard her father talking to her mother about an Indian chief who helped the British in fighting for freedom. She quickly walked into the kitchen and joined her parents at the kitchen table.

"Sometimes you have to fight to keep the things that belong to you, and to see that justice is done," her father said.

His face looked serious, and his smooth brown skin seemed to reflect the lamplight in a strange way as he talked. Maybe that's the way the Indian chief's skin looked when he was sitting by the campfire at night preparing his battle plans, Jana thought. Then her father's face began to look happy again, and his voice sounded happy when he said that some time they should all take a day off and make a trip to the sites where the battle took place and the Indian

Village was burned.

One morning in late summer, Jana's father and mother told her they had a surprise for her. They were all going on a picnic. They were going to see where the Moravian village was burned by the Americans. And they were going to see the big monument built for Tecumseh.

Tecumseh, her father explained, was a Shawnee Indian chief who came up from the American Colonies to help the British fight against the American invaders in the War of 1812. The Americans were defeated, but Tecumseh was killed in the battle. The Indians would not tell where they buried the great chief.

As they drove through the reservation that morning, and out into the wider white people's land, it seemed that the world was composed of different shades of green: from the soft green of the trees, to the rich green of the sumach, to the dark green of the corn (hurrying to get ripe before the frost, her mother said). Only the wheat seemed to be a different colour. It was like the gold in her mother's locket. It must have looked like that when the Americans burned the village, her father said.

They parked the car near the monument in the park on the river bank. Some trees showed slight tinges of yellow. It was easy for the imagination to see touches of red, which would soon be there to announce the coming of Indian summer. The dry grass behind the monument looked soft and warm in the mellow noonday light.

"I wish we could have brought Kathleen," Jana remarked, eyeing the soft grass.

She had missed her best friend when she went away to the Academy. When she came home on holidays, they soon became best friends again. They often hid away behind the thorn bushes and told stories, and sang silly songs as they lay on their backs looking up at the blue sky.

"Why?" her mother asked.

"Then we could lie in the grass. Lying in the long grass is like being in the place you were in before you were born, Kathleen said. You are safe and warm, and you don't have to worry about anything."

"Kathleen seems to be more sensitive than most girls her age," her mother remarked.

"Can I lie down in the warm grass after lunch, mother?" Jana asked.

"No, dear, you might get grass stains on your

pretty dress. The grass does look inviting though, doesn't it?" her mother asked, directing a peculiar smile at Jana's father. Her father nodded and squeezed her mother's hand a little. He looked up at the flag waving in the late August breeze.

"Tecumseh gave his blood for freedom," her father said. He stood looking at the flag for some time. "Tecumseh blood in 1813. Hillman blood one hundred years later!"

Jana turned to the monument. "Look at the turtle!"

"Where?" Her mother scanned the grass of the river bank.

"There." Jana pointed to the monument.

"Tecumseh's mother's Indian name," her mother remarked, in surprise.

"Turtle laying eggs in the sand," Jana read.

"Indian names have meanings," her father explained. "It was a way to identify individuals. Sometimes white names have meaning too, but we don't think much about that any more. It doesn't seem important."

"Some people still think they have a degree of importance because they carry a particular name," her mother remarked. "But it's not the name that carries the importance. It's the quality of the person that carries that."

"Tecumseh?" Jana questioned. Her mother nodded, and reached into the basket for the corn soup.

"It's still hot," she said, ladling out three generous portions. "Tecumseh ate corn soup too, you know. Hot soup, hot tea and sandwiches. That should satisfy the great chief."

After lunch, Jana and her parents walked along the river to the site where the Indian village stood before the Americans burned it. There were markers indicating the locations of the Indian houses. The markers showed that some of the Indians had adopted the names of the Moravian missionaries.

Below the village, near the river, was the place where Tecumseh was supposed to have fallen as he tried to escape from the Americans.

The forested area around the village was quiet and peaceful now. It was hard for Jana to imagine the roar of cannons, and the crack of rifle fire from the tree tops, and men on both sides bleeding and dying right where she stood with her parents.

The man at the museum said it was true. He showed them arrowheads, and heavy cannon balls and rifle bullets. They had been recovered from the battle ground and from the river, he said. He showed them some bullets and cannon balls that were made from stone.

The two-mile walk to the village, and the two miles back, had made Jana thirsty. She quickly drank the glass of lemonade her mother gave her.

She looked again at the soft grass as she stretched and yawned. "I'd still like to lie down in that warm nest," she said.

"Come," her mother called. "The sun will have dropped behind the palisades by the time our wagon reaches the fort."

"Oh, Mother..."

"Just a little corn soup humour. Remember, I live on a reservation." She glanced at the sun, redder and larger now, as it accelerated toward the western horizon.

"'Oh, great fiery orb which giveth life...' I seem to have forgotten most of my poetry," her mother said. She swung the basket over her arm and started to turn, then stopped abruptly, as her eyes fell upon two thin streaks of red on the maples across the river.

"'Swift my canoe on a silver stream, With scarlet lace to hold my dream.' Maybe I should have been a poet...or a musician." She turned back to Jana.

"That reminds me...you have an hour of piano to do before it's time to tuck you in with the 'winkin,' blinkin' and nods.'" Her mother had not forgotten the nursery rhyme which was so often her companion when she tucked Jana in and kissed her goodnight. Jana was too old for that now, but it was still nice to think about.

"In a week I will no longer be tucking you in. Your den mother at the Academy will again have that privilege. Sometimes.... But if you're going to amount to something, you're going to have to be properly educated. And you'll be home for Christmas. We can look forward to that, even if we can't look forward to you being a teenager." She pulled Jana to her, and gave her a pat on the behind as she spun her around.

Jana skipped back to the monument and traced her finger around the turtle cut into the stone on Tecumseh's monument.

"I want to remember what the turtle looks like, so I can draw it in art class," she told her mother. She smiled when she thought of the reactions the drawing might bring. Some of the girls would likely call it abstract art. She would try to explain to them why it was authentic. She thought many of the girls would know about Tecumseh.

"Father, was Tecumseh...? Oh! he has fallen asleep in the warm grass, Mother."

"He seems to be falling asleep at odd times lately. Perhaps he's working too hard. We'll let him rest a little before we start for home."

"They say Tecumseh was a different kind of Indian. Was he, mother?"

"Shawnee...he was a Shawnee from the south, as your father mentioned."

"Am I Shawnee?"

"No, dear."

"What am I?"

"You're half-Scotch and Norwegian, and half-Delaware Indian."

"Then I'm not Indian; I'm not white...I'm not anything!"

"Indeed you are something...something to be proud of." She pulled the girl to her, tightening her arm around her waist. "I'm proud of you. Some day the world will be proud of you. I can feel that to the very core of my being." Her mother laughed and loosened her hold. "I haven't said that...I haven't felt.... It's funny how we use those words. Until now I've thought of them mostly...I don't know...when I'm listening to great music - music that reaches to the very depths of my conscious reality." She stopped walking, and seemed to be pondering her words.

"Grieg must have experienced feelings that deeply. How else could he have written music which reaches right into people's hearts?"

"Was he part-Indian?"

"No, he was half-Scotch and half-Norwegian like me. He was a great composer. His music is heart to heart."

Jana's brow furrowed, as she struggled to understand what her mother meant.

"Did I ever tell you that when your father and I were married, I had the pianist play Grieg's *Wedding day at Troldhaugen?* At most weddings the organist played Mendelssohn's *Wedding March,* or the standard *Here Comes the Bride* from Wagner's Lohengrin. I wanted something different!

"I wonder if Grieg's Viking ancestors had some of those same feelings he had. If they did, they probably thought they came from the northern lights. They were a superstitious lot. Perhaps their strange stories compensated for their lack of music. They say that some of those stories are still read in the original dialect in Iceland.

"It's frightening to think of not being able to express thoughts that are in the heart." A deeply pensive look spread over her face. "Grieg makes me proud of my heritage."

"Should I be proud of my herit...?"

"Heritage. It's what you inherited from your parents, and their parents, and your culture. It's mostly the qualities of mind and body you came into the world with."

"But should I be proud?"

"Only of what's noble about you. That's all. False pride destroys the noble elements within us." Her mother's face still wore a slightly serious look as she turned slowly toward the car.

Jana searched for something to please her. "Tonight, after practice, I'm going to shine up my room so you won't have to do it when I leave. And tomorrow, I'm going to help you to wash all the clothes I'll need at the Academy," she said.

"Well, that is...rather noble, I'd say." Her mother laughed, and the good colour came back to her face.

IV

"Young ladies, I'm your new social studies teacher. My name is Miss Hedley. Laura Hedley."

"Good morning, Miss Hedley."

Two older girls behind Jana began to whisper as soon as the teacher told them her name. "If that's the way she always dresses, no wonder she's a 'miss,'" one girl remarked. Miss Hedley seemed to hear them, even if she couldn't understand the exact words. The teacher's face sobered, and Jana knew Miss Hedley was going to say something she had not intended to say.

"Each of you take a piece of paper," Miss Hedley ordered, her voice controlled and quiet. "I will recite ten questions which have, in total, twenty parts. Here is an example: 'Name two important Arctic explorers.' What would your answer be?"

Her question was greeted with complete silence.

"Apparently it is of little or no importance to have knowledge of such things, or surely some one of you would have an answer." Miss Hedley looked straight at the class. A slightly cynical smile spread across her face, coaxing the colour back.

"I'll state each question once. I might as well grasp the opportunity to apply some lessons in Economics. Economy in the use of words. Economy in the use of energy. Economy in the use of time. My policy this term will stress economy in those areas.

"Here are the questions: 'Name two Canadian scientists. Name two Canadian poets. Name two Canadian prime ministers. Name two Canadian composers. Name two great Canadian painters. Name two great Canadian rivers.'" When she completed the questions, she instructed each girl to pass her paper to the girl in front of her for marking.

"Here is a list of acceptable answers," Miss Hedley stated. She let her gaze move slowly across the room. "It is of little use to continue this project. By now you will all have discovered your level of competence. To pursue the project further would prove embarrassing to some of you. Embarrassing individuals is not on my list of priorities. It is harmful, and seldom accomplishes anything."

Jana detected a quiet sobbing behind her. It gradually became audible across the room.

"You may leave the room if you wish," Miss Hedley said to the crying girl and glanced at her wrist watch. "Heavens. I spoke of economy in the use of time, and suddenly we have no time left. Hurry now, or you will be late for literature. It's Burns' poetry today, I understand. Ah...'A man's a man for ah that.'" Miss Hedley laughed this time, and Jana thought she could detect a little bit of mischief in her deep brown eyes.

As Jana was leaving, she glanced at Miss Hedley's dress. It could use some colour, she thought. Indian summer colour.

It was the music classes Jana liked best. Mr. Neilson seemed happy most all the time. He made them work very hard, but he treated them well. He never raised his voice, except when he got excited about a certain piano concerto or some ballet music by Chopin.

She liked the ballet music too. It helped to hear Miss Broome's pianist playing it when they were stretching to do the hard steps. Without the music, she was sure she could never do some of the muscle-pulling exercises.

She thought she was starting to feel some of the things in music her mother talked about. Maybe it was in her heart, like her mother said...like Grieg felt, and wrote into his music so other hearts could feel it.

You should learn to balance so delicately, that the "tinkle of a breaking wine glass could blow you over," her teacher said. And sometimes, you should feel the music going into every part of your body. That's when the music was saying to your body and spirit: "Hey...wake up! This is life!"

Sometimes when classes were over, Jana was so tired she just wanted to take a deep breath and collapse in a puddle on the floor. But you could never do that until you first went to Miss Broome and reached out your hand and said, "Good After-noon, Miss Broome."

Miss Broome told Jana that she had wonderful hair for combing back in ballet-style, and that she had a rich shade of skin and a lovely nordic profile. It was a classical look, Miss Broome said. Jana didn't know exactly what that meant, but it pleased Miss Broome, and she was glad for that.

Wandering back to her dormitory one after-noon from ballet, Jana thought she was too tired to eat supper. She didn't seem to need food, anyway. Her whole body and mind were so packed with music and dancing and words and thoughts, that there wasn't much room for anything else. But she had to maintain proper nutrition, Miss Broome said.

As she walked slowly toward the dining room, she thought of the squirrels at the edge of the forest. She wondered how they would like the music the pianist played in Miss Broome's classes for their silly, squirrel ballet. Would they be able to feel the music all over, the way she was starting to? Maybe they heard a kind of squirrel music when they ran and skipped with their mouths full of cones, or when they soared from tree to tree. Did a squirrel have a spirit like she had? Did animals really have spirits?

Time passed quickly the second year. Still, there were times when Jana felt a painful longing for home. And sometimes she thought she would give up everything if she could only see her mother and father for a little while. Sometimes, she could not hold back her tears.

Her loneliness must be something like the lone-liness her ballet teacher talked about, she reasoned. "None but the lonely heart..." Miss Broome said. "Those words by Tschaikovsky are meant to come from...they could only come from a woman's heart. You must be able to express her emotion in the way you move. Otherwise your exercises are bland and quite meaningless.

"You see, our lives are made up of a series of experiences, and those experiences are always ac-companied by emotions of some sort: sometimes loneliness, sometimes sorrow, sometimes anger (I hope you will not let that emotion be predominant), sometimes great joy - joy so intense that it is difficult to contain oneself. A time when the heart is gloriously in harmony with the whole world about us, a time when we are swept up into the radiance of our spiritual being. It is the most powerful emotion of all."

When Miss Broome talked that way about joy, it seemed to drain her of every ounce of energy.

"You will soon be reaching an age when emotional elements of your nature will be making themselves known more profoundly than you can now imagine. How beautiful it will be when those emotions shine brilliantly in your dance!"

The human heart was the station in the body where all the great emotions came together, Miss Broome said.

It was only two weeks after Miss Broome talked about emotions that Jana woke very early one morning with some new feelings. This time the feelings weren't in the heart. They were in another part of her body, and they were causing her real concern. Her mother said something would happen the day she left her at the railway station. It was part of being a girl. "Don't worry," she said. "When it does happen, scoot right down to the nurse's office. She'll take care of you."

Jana quickly washed her face, brushed her teeth and put on a clean dress. She was waiting at the door when the nurse came to her office.

"Good Afternoon."

A questioning look came to the nurse's normally placid countenance.

"I beg your pardon?"

"I'm sorry...I'm very sorry. It's 'Good Morning' I should have said." Momentarily she had associated what Miss Broome said about emotions, with the practice of saying "Good Afternoon" when the class began and ended. The nurse looked at her moist eyes.

"It's easy to get a bit flustered and disoriented when there's something bothering us, isn't it? Especially when it's personal. Come with me, my girl, and we'll see if we can find the nasty little gremlin that's mixing up the time zones between my office and the dormitory!"

After the examination, the nurse pronounced her normal and healthy, then put something down in her book. "Please come and see me any time. Don't worry." She turned her eyes to the window and looked high in the sky. "That blue dome looks as secure as it did when I was a little girl. There were some people at that time who told us the sky was falling. I never believed them."

The examinations at the end of the school year were much more difficult than Jana had anticipated, especially the history, geography and mathematics. She trembled in the silence of the examination hall as she struggled to find a way to put down the correct answers in history, at the same time preserving what she thought to be the truth.

History seemed to present people like her father in a less favourable light than it did the white settlers. The word "savages" crept into the stories of conquest. She couldn't imagine her father being the type of person who would scalp the white people.

She had never been able to tell for certain how Mr. Carpenter felt when he talked about justice for all people. She could feel his awareness of her presence in the history classes. Sometimes he seemed uncomfortable with what he had to teach from the text book.

Geography gave her, for the first time, an appreciation of the distribution of the land. The white people had most of the land, while the Indians were confined to reservations spread across the length and breadth of the country.

Mathematics gave her much to be concerned

about. But she knew she must persevere. "The rewards belong to those who persevere," her mother said.

Maybe the Indians didn't persevere enough, Jana thought.

V

"Your father is ill," her mother said, after she embraced Jana on the railway station platform. "I thought it best to wait until your exams were over to tell you."

Jana looked closely at her mother. That beautifully shaped mouth had kissed her a thousand times. And her Scotch-red hair always fell onto her face when her mother bent down to kiss her.

Now her mother did not have to bend down, for Jana was almost as tall as her mother, and she stood straight like her mother. She wondered why her mother had not kissed her. She wanted to reach out and touch her mother's fine, pale skin, as she had often done as a child.

"He is seriously ill," her mother continued, and now she reached forward and kissed Jana lightly on the cheek. "I'm happy you're home," she said, forcing a smile. "We'll have to manage somehow. There's much to do. Perhaps we could hire a young man to help. He would have to be strong and reliable - someone we could count on."

Jana drew her mother close to her.

"I'm proud of you, my girl." Her mother released her firm grip on her hand. "I guess I don't need to lead you along with me anymore. It's a bit painful seeing you grow up, and not wanting you to grow up. We are strangely complex, aren't we...? The human species, I mean."

Her mother was beginning to relax. She was quickly becoming the mother she left standing on that station platform, six months earlier. Jana pressed her foot down firmly on the solid planks. It was good to be home.

"We'll go to see your father before going back to the farm," her mother stated.

The doctor had the diagnosis ready for them when they reached the Thames General Hospital.

"Polio," the doctor said. "I'm sorry. Several cases have shown up here in the last three months. Some are extremely serious. Some are rather mild. Your husband, unfortunately is in the first category, Mrs. Hillman. I must be forthright with you. The prognosis is not good." He hesitated. "We'll do the best we can for him here. There are no cures."

Jana fainted.

When Jana opened her eyes, her mother's mouth was set in a little smile, and she was holding her hand.

"For a moment I thought you had deserted me," her mother said.

Jana tried to tell her that she wanted to go home, but her weak voice could form only barely audible words.

"We're going to drive through the country on the way home," her mother said. "It's a lovely day for a drive. They say there are some apples ripe enough for a pie. I'll slip in and see your father once more before we leave. Just lie still, and I'll be right back."

Jana lay quietly on the stretcher the orderly had brought into the small room off the doctor's office. The afternoon sun was starting to come in through the window, warming her legs. She began to think of the drive through the country in the warm sunshine. And the apples her mother talked about. Apple pie!

She could almost smell the sweet, tart aroma of new apples as their syrupy juice bubbled from the edges of the golden crust when her mother took the pie from the oven.

The car turned the corner from behind a woodlot. Before them lay a large orchard stretching away to the north and east. Green apples, bright and firm, hung thick among the leaves in the warm sun urging them to maturity. Occasionally there was a tree with apples of greenish-cream colour, and there were a few trees with apples already showing blushes of red.

"This is the place, I believe," Mrs. Hillman said. She turned the car into the laneway toward the house.

Two boys were coming out of the orchard with a basket of apples, whose red blushes flashed in the sunshine.

"They're not quite mature yet," her mother said, as they got out of the car.

"One of them looks mature."

"No, Jana, I mean the apples. They're not quite mature." As the boys approached the house her mother called out, "Are those apples for sale?"

"No," the younger boy said. He looked at the older boy.

"They could be, maybe," the older boy remarked.

"They're for Mother," the younger boy insisted.

"She told us to pick them when she left for the berry patch this morning."

"We could find some more that are ripe enough," the older boy stated.

"Well, what will your decision be?" her mother asked.

"They are for sale," the older boy said firmly.

"Very well. How much are they?"

"I...I don't know...you can give me whatever you think they're worth."

"How about a dollar?"

"That's too much. Nobody ever pays that much."

"Well, I think it would be a fair price for these beautiful apples. I'm sure they make lovely pies."

"They do!" the younger boy exclaimed. "That's why Mother wants them here when she gets home."

"It looks as though you two have some more work to do. Is it hard work?"

"Not very," the older boy said. "Not half as hard as picking up potatoes and pitching hay and threshing and things like that."

"Do you work at all those things?"

"Sure."

"Do you ever work away from home?"

"Sometimes."

Her mother brought her index finger lightly to her chin. "Are you free...would you be willing to work for me? It's some distance. You would not be able to come home at night. You would have to live with us."

"I'll go," the boy said.

Jana peered closely at the boy. He seemed rather shy, she thought, but he was nice-looking, with wavy, black hair. Her mother was taking quick looks at his hands and nodding, as she did unconsciously when she approved of something. The boy looked at Jana twice, but there was no indication that he saw her as anything but another young teenager. And if he noticed her light brown skin, he never showed it.

"Do you go to school?" her mother asked. He smiled, sensing that she thought school was important.

"I finished grade ten this year," he said proudly.

"Can you be at the mission farm on the reservation at eight o'clock Monday morning?"

"Yes." He looked slightly puzzled.

"Do we live on the reservation?" she said, sensing his curiosity. "Yes, we do. Are you still prepared to come to work for us?"

"Sure," the boy said emphatically. The younger boy looked up at him with unbelieving eyes.

"Very well. I will ask Enoch to instruct you. He's getting quite elderly, but I'm sure he'll agree to help us out for a while."

Mrs. Hillman reached out her hand to him. He hesitantly took her hand in his, then let it slip easily away.

"My name is Glen, and my brother's name is Ted."

"I'm Mrs. Hillman. My daughter's name is Jana."

VI

The mission farm spread out in a flat, clay plain leaning to the river. For years, its good soil had produced bountiful crops, and sustained the Moravians who came to teach the white man's religion and agriculture to a hunting and fishing culture.

All that was left of the great missionary enterprise was an old church and a few farm buildings. Some broken tombstones leaning against the church were testimony to the dreams of the missionaries which went with them to their graves.

When Roy Hillman rented the farm from the Mission Convention, it was covered with scrub trees and bushes which threatened to return the land to wilderness.

After a few years, the land became productive again. It provided a good living for Roy Hillman and his new bride. And it provided work for some of the Indians living nearby.

As Glen let his eyes scan the wide expanse of land in the softness of early morning, his dreams of going to school to become an engineer, or a doctor, seemed closer to fulfillment. He might even become a great doctor, like the old doctor his mother named him after. Mrs. Hillman said that eventually he might take charge and share in the profits of the mission farm.

When he became a doctor or an engineer, he'd get his mother one of the new washing machines that had a little engine to do the work. She wouldn't be scrubbing the skin off her knuckles on the washboard anymore, or wringing the clothes by hand. And he'd pay off the last of the mortgage so she'd never get kicked out onto the road again.

The missionaries and their Indian students must have worked hard to carve this great farm out of the forest, Glen thought. He would work hard. That land would sustain him. It would educate him.

"Glen, Enoch is here. Please come and be introduced. Then he will get you started."

Enoch had clean clothes, and he was clean-shaven. His deep-set eyes peered out from a mild face. Enoch was never satisfied just looking to the boundaries of the reservation, Mrs. Hillman said. He was the kind of Indian whose eyes looked out into the world, and they saw a part of life most of the others missed. He had been a steady worker, mostly on the mission farm, but the land had never enslaved his mind as it had his body: "Pulled my mind down into the soil," Enoch said.

Enoch turned his eyes from Mrs. Hillman to Glen. He stood looking at him for a moment, then said something in a strange language, with no change in the puzzled expression on his face.

"It's Delaware," he told Mrs. Hillman. "It means: 'I think we will discover each other's thoughts, and we will be pleased.'" Mrs. Hillman smiled and hurried toward the house.

"Dinner at twelve o'clock." The sharp report of the screen door lent emphasis to her words.

"Can you drive a tractor?" Enoch asked, as they

approached the large machinery shed.

"Yes...I..." Enoch turned slowly toward him, his grey eyes now close, and questioning. "I mean...I haven't really driven one, but I watched when the fruit farmer drove his, and I know I can do it."

Enoch stood motionless for a moment at the door to the shed.

"There is no word in Delaware for tractor," he said, and pushed open the sliding door. "The land shows impatience today," he remarked.

If the land was impatient, Glen's impatience was ready to match it. He threw himself into the work with such determination that there was little time for anything else in his life. He resented anything which got in his way, and he found himself becoming short-tempered at times.

He didn't like milking the two cows which provided milk and cream for the mission farm. He thought Jana could be doing that, but he was afraid to make the suggestion. She probably didn't know how to do it anyway. If she did, likely Enoch would have told him, now that they talked comfortably about things, including Jana, occasionally.

One evening when Glen was milking, Jana came to

the stable. She watched the fast streams of milk being directed into the shiny pail, making a kind of musical sound when they hit the sides.

"It's rather amazing, isn't it?" she said. "'Milk, the food of life.'"

"It would be more amazing..." Glen caught himself before he said something about her not offering to help.

"Do you think we're parasites?"

He turned to her with a puzzled look.

"I mean, do you think we are parasites living off another species...cows, for instance?"

"I've never thought about that. One thing I do know...you don't live off them without work."

"Maybe the cows are parasites living off us," she ventured.

His tired hands would easily agree with that suggestion, he thought.

"Maybe we are all parasites," she suggested. "We prey on each other, it seems to me. We try to satisfy our wants and needs by taking what we want, sometimes taking from another person. Don't you agree?"

"I'm finished," he said, stripping the last of the milk, then rising slowly from the stool.

"I'll help you to take the milk to the house," she

said. "Maybe I should learn to milk so I could help you."

He could feel his fatigue beginning to lessen as they started toward the house. They balanced the full pail between them, each with a hand on the handle.

"Father liked drinking the warm milk right from the cow," Jana said, looking down at the swaying milk. "I wish Mother and I could take him some when we go to see him on the weekend."

VII

After a few weeks, Jana began to come often to the stable when Glen was milking.

One night, as he undressed, he thought of her. He stood naked for some time, then fell onto the bed in a delicious helplessness.

He worried that Mrs. Hillman might sense the change in his behaviour toward Jana and question him about it. She might even suggest that he look for another job.

One Friday evening Jana came to the stable carrying a glass pitcher.

"Please?" she said, with a mischievous smile. "Mother needs two cups extra for the birthday cake she's making for Father. She wants it to be large enough for all the patients in the ward."

"Oh, sure." He filled the pitcher from the half-full pail.

"I've heard that cows kick. Do they?"

"Sometimes."

"Why?"

For a moment he was without an answer.

"Some of them are just mean, that's all."

"Have you ever been kicked?"

"Twice."

"Did it hurt?"

"One time it did, when the cow kicked me so hard I somersaulted backwards off the stool."

"Why did she do it?"

"It was real cold. I was in a hurry to get to school."

"Oh, she was angry because you wouldn't take her to school," she teased.

"My cold hands," he said, turning away from her.

"You mean you put your cold hands on her...?"

"Yes."

"I don't blame that cow a bit! I'd kick too if

somebody...Oh, I must get this milk to Mother." She started for the house, then stopped and turned. "I've heard that cows like music. Have you ever heard that?"

"Yeah, the old guy near us plays a radio from his car battery when he's milking, and when..."

"When?"

"When he wants to get the heifers...when it's time to..."

"To what?"

He hesitated.

"To breed them?"

"Yes," he answered curtly.

"I've got to go," she said.

VIII

The summer had gone. The reds of the sumach, and the yellows of hardwoods marked the fence rows and woodlots, and a mellow softness lay over the land.

Glen watched Jana walking toward him as he pushed the doors of the machinery shed closed for the night. She seemed to have grown a foot over the summer. Her whole body moved in a flexible and graceful rhythm.

"Mother has arranged for a small musical concert this evening," she called before she got to him. "There will be just us three, and Enoch. Do you like classical music?" When she saw his hesitation, she said, "Don't worry, I'll play something for you on the piano if you don't like the recordings."

He was ashamed to tell her that he was only familiar with the old-time music he played on his fiddle.

Glen glanced at the faces of Jana and Mrs. Hillman as they sat quietly listening to a violin concerto which was totally unfamiliar to him.

There was something in both their faces he had not seen before. They seemed to be in a kind of spell.

Several times his attention lapsed, and he started to find reasons for not listening any longer. But he disciplined himself and directed his attention back to the music. Eventually, it did not seem to be such an effort to maintain his concentration and if his attention drifted away momentarily, it came back easily. After a few minutes, the music seemed to be more inviting, and even to be subtly suggesting that he might join with the others.

As he continued to listen, he began to follow particular strains, thinking that might lead him more directly to whatever it was that was holding Jana and her mother - and Enoch - in a kind of hypnotic state.

He closed his eyes. As he kept listening, he began to feel a faint desire stirring in him for more understanding, for more appreciation, and pleasure.

It was frightening to think of leaving the security of the old music. He could feel the new music starting to urge him toward another dimension. It promised understanding and satisfaction; it promised an experience more profound than any music had ever allowed him. His pulse quickened, yet his heart remained placid. Suddenly he felt his mind being driven toward the limit of its emotional boundaries. His body trembled as he contemplated the strange and frightening world he was approaching. Was that what Jana meant by music and goose bumps? Was that what she meant by music of the heart?

When the music stopped, he opened his eyes to confirm that he was still in a normal world.

"I'll play you a little Chopin on the piano while Mother is getting the coffee," Jana said. "Not the hard stuff, just a little of the ballet music. It's called *Les Sylphides.* Isn't that a nice title? It sounds exactly right for ballet."

He watched her as she let her long fingers dance over the keys. The music, so different from the violin concerto, had a delight and freedom about it. Again he felt himself being pulled farther away from the simple music he had known. He was a little ashamed, for he felt he was leaving the old music for good - music which had been his life-long friend.

He thought of the poem about the two forks in the road. Once you chose a road you could never go back. That's the way it was with an evolving species, his biology teacher said, and that's the way it was with people.

"You seemed to be dreaming," Jana said. "I was watching from the corner of my eye. I was almost afraid to stop playing. What were you thinking?"

"Oh, I...it's a little hard to explain. It's just something I never had to think about before."

"I shouldn't be asking you, anyway."

"It's okay." His eyes followed her as she walked to the table to pour the coffee. Her face was radiant under the light of the hanging lamp. The warm light washed over her bare neck and shoulders, and bathed the soft silhouettes of her firm breasts.

The light caught Jana's eyes as she turned toward him. Traces of the music magic he had seen a few minutes earlier were still there.

She was the most beautiful girl he had ever seen. And that beauty flowed right into her soul. He was sure of that. He wanted to get up and take her in his arms to tell her that he loved her...that he would....

"This is for you," Jana said, holding out a cup of coffee for him.

His hand trembled as he reached for the cup.

She smiled at him. "Are you all right now?"

He nodded his head.

"Music affects Enoch profoundly," Jana said. Her voice was almost a whisper. "Did you know that he had his own dance band when he was young? He played both saxophone and clarinet. You seem surprised."

"I am. I thought he would have told me."

"Will you walk Enoch home tonight?" she asked. "Mother doesn't want him on the road alone with that gang of boys looking for mischief."

"Sure."

"By the way, Mother asked Jimmy to come for two days to help you when the bean threshers come.

You look pleased."

"It's like getting a warm spring shower at the right time," Glen said. Jimmy worked as hard as he did, and he came on time, not like some of the Indian boys who showed up when they felt like it. Jimmy was different in lots of ways. He was "going to amount to something," Jimmy kept telling him. "You already amount to something," he told him.

He had come to that conclusion when Jimmy jumped into the river to save those two kids from town who knew nothing about handling a canoe.

Jimmy was fishing with his rolling net down river where he could hide the tow cable in the bushes. When he heard the boys screaming, Jimmy let go of the cable, and the net rolled back into the river. He ran toward the screams and jumped fully clothed into the cold water. He grabbed the two boys' coat sleeves in one hand and towed them to shore. "The current damn near got them," he said. "The current and the cold water damn near got me too."

The next morning when he asked Jimmy about the rolling net, Jimmy said it was likely halfway to the lake by then. He'd soon make another one. "I'll be damned if I'm going to let all those fresh pickerel get away."

"Oft in the darkness of night, I have ventured forth

beyond the palisades and arrived safely at my dwelling," Enoch said, half-seriously.

Jana smiled.

"Ah, but now the gang instinct rules that road at night," Mrs. Hillman replied.

"Thank you," Enoch said. "Goodnight."

As they walked beyond the limits of the house lights, Glen struggled to find conversation which might be appropriate. But Enoch determined what they would talk about.

"Some of the young people are becoming violent in their actions and in their words," Enoch said. "Did Jana tell you how they abuse her?"

"No."

"Some of the people, mostly the boys, have resented her because she's half-white and because her father has done well. Some of the comments have been cruel, even from the time she was a child."

"She never said anything."

"'Little Miss Rich Bitch!' That's what they called her, even when she attended the mission school with the other children. It got worse when she came home from the Academy for holidays. Bad jokes. It bothered me and I'd take them to task sometimes. But that never stopped them. They even suggested that I should keep clear of them." Enoch hesitated. "You now know the reason for Mrs. Hillman's concern."

"I'm sorry."

"They got at Jana and her father too, with one bad joke. You'll likely hear it if you're here long enough. They resent her father for being progressive."

Surely Jana could handle that, Glen reckoned. Still, the thought of any kind of abuse directed at her made him feel uncomfortable and angry.

"I thought it might be proper to inform you of these unpleasant things. It saddens me to see what's happening to some of our people. I understand how these attitudes came about. There was some justification. But many of the Indians have enslaved themselves, and they will never be free just by damning the white man and not looking beyond that."

Glen didn't know what to say. He remembered the history teacher seeming uneasy with having to teach what was in the textbook.

"They have cut themselves off." Enoch paused, looking through the darkness toward the river. "One day, after I turned seventeen, I wandered into the world of my mind. I liked that, and I started to do it often. I discovered some good things. Music was one of them. I saved my money and bought a clarinet, then a saxophone. Soon I had my own band - an 'Indian Band,'" he chuckled. "I was only nineteen. The war was on.

"When I came back, I got the band organized again. We played mostly for dances, but there were concerts, too. Some nights, after working in the field all day, I thought I'd never be able to blow a note on the clarinet. Once I heard the good sound, my energy came flowing back. It was another world, you see. There's another world out there for us. There was for me. It's still there.

"When I went to the fields to labour, I never let the earth enslave my mind, as it did my body."

Glen could not make out the expression on Enoch's face in the light of the rising harvest moon, but he was sure it wore that slow, philosophical smile.

"A few more steps." Enoch tapped his cane in time with his step. "There are always a few more steps we can take, if our desire and determination are in harmony with each other."

Glen stepped quickly from the short lane to the gravel road, which was now a pale, grey line winding through two strips of dense vegetation still holding the darkness. He could hear a screech owl in the distance.

It was a dangerous time for mice and moles. The owl, which identified itself so vocally, would soon be so quiet in a death dive that the mice and moles, and even the nesting sparrows, would not detect it in time to escape its deadly talons. Glen felt sorry for the small animals and birds, whose lives were snuffed out in an instant by a killer in the night.

The owl proclaimed its territory again. This time its call fell unevenly on his ears. Perhaps it was a young owl whose voice was not mature, he thought. He stopped and listened carefully.

It was not an owl. It was an imitation, and it was moving closer to him. He shivered. The 'gang' they had talked about. What were they up to? Would they attack him, or just try to frighten him?

He could see figures darting across the road into the dark vegetation. He clenched his fists.

Suddenly a chorus of piercing yells greeted him. Figures ran into the open, then leapt back into the undergrowth. Their yells were interspersed with lewd comments. "Her old man named Little Miss Rich Bitch ninety-nine, because she was always under a buck!"

Glen kept walking until he was opposite his adversaries. He could see that most of them were smaller than he was. Still, there were a half-dozen of them, and he'd be no match for them. He might take out two, maybe even three, but the others would surely pounce on him.

As he hurried by, a hail of gravel slammed against his body, stinging his face and his bare hands as he tried to protect his eyes.

The assault ended abruptly.

"That's only a warning." It was an older gang member's voice. "Next time, look out. You know what we might do, if you keep on coming to our reserve? We might use our scalping knives. And when we're finished, you'll be missing some important parts - the parts that make you a boy, the parts you're saving for Little Miss Rich Bitch!" A roar of taunting laughter rose from the gang, followed by high-pitched wails.

Glen's fists flailed at them as they ducked out of the way and scattered. He was still screaming as the last of them plunged into the dark vegetation.

His heart gradually slowed, and he stood perfectly still for a few seconds, waiting to be sure it was over. He had lost his self-control and it happened almost instantly. It was a lesson he would have to remember. Still, he had stood up to them, and that was compensation of a sort for his loss of discipline.

Jana was looking out from the screen door.
"Trouble?"
"A little."
"I thought so. I'm sorry."
"It's all right."
Jana opened the door and stepped out into the yard. The orange light from the harvest moon lay softly on her face and cast an aura around her shining hair. He wanted to fall into the arms of the beautiful girl before him; he wanted to feel the beat of her heart, telling him everything would be fine, as he lay his head on her breast and drifted into sleep.

"You're wounded," she said. "There's blood on your face."
"It's nothing."
She went into the house and returned with a wet washcloth. She gently cleaned the blood and grit from his face. "I think it will be all right." She put her finger tips to his shoulder and moved him into the house.

"You'd better keep that washcloth handy for Jimmy and me when we come out of that threshing barn tomorrow night," he joked. "We'll be covered with an inch of black dirt."

She smiled, and said it was getting late.

"There was a call from the hospital," she said, looking toward the hanging lamp. "It's Father. The time is very short. Mother went right to bed after the call."

Jimmy was pounding on the door before Glen was out of bed.

Glen pulled on his shirt and went downstairs. "What's wrong, Jimmy?" he asked through the screen door.

"Come out!" Jimmy called.

Glen stepped through the door, closing it behind him.

"Jimmy?"

"Last night!" Jimmy blurted out. "I know what happened! They woke me up. They were sitting in that old wrecked car in the alley behind our house, blowing about what they did to you. I could hear every word. I grabbed my pants and went out."

"They didn't do me any harm."

"Not this time, but wait till next time. Those young bastards might kill you if they're hopped up on that rotten moonshine that son-of-a-bitch of a bootlegger gets for them."

"Oh, Jimmy, I..."

"They'll be too damned scared to try that stuff again, as long as I'm around," Jimmy declared.

Jimmy's words made sense. Jimmy was bigger than most of the Indian boys, and he had a powerfully-built body which he kept in perfect condition. It would take a lot of guts for anyone to tackle Jimmy.

"What did you do, Jimmy...when you went out?"

"I surprised them by coming at them from behind the shed. They didn't have time to get away. Noah froze right in his seat. Bertrand was halfway through that broken window when I grabbed his shirt and pulled it tight around his neck. He started to choke, so I loosened it a bit. Then I told them, 'If you bastards ever touch Glen, or cause any trouble for Mrs. Hillman, I'll choke you till your damn tongues hang out and I'll beat the hell out of you so bad you'll wish you were dead.' I choked Bertrand again, to make sure he knew what I meant. Then I hauled Noah out of the seat. He got lippy with me, so I gave him a damn good backhand across the mouth, and when he started to run, I kicked his ass good."

The black dust whirled out of the threshing machine in a thick blanket, completely surrounding them as they forked the tinder-dry beans in steady rhythm into its hungry maw. They choked and spat, and their parched throats cracked from the steady assault of dust and grit. No amount of water could lessen the punishment for long, and as Glen's throat threatened to break open and bleed, he longed for the end of the day.

Jimmy fared better. He said it was the chewing tobacco. It gathered the dust in his mouth and made it easier on the throat. When the absorption of the tobacco juice reached a certain stage, you just spat it out. Glen had been tempted to try it. Finally Jimmy asked if he was ready.

"Don't take too big a bite." Jimmy handed him the plug. It stung Glen's tongue, and he almost spat it out.

"Stick it between your lower teeth and your lip. You just need a little of the juice now and then, to gather the dust."

Soon Glen's whole mouth felt as though it were on fire.

"I can't do it. I'm sorry to waste it."

He spat out the disgusting brown wad onto a structural post, away from the beans.

"It takes a little practice," Jimmy said, chewing.

The dust filled Glen's throat and nostrils, and stung his eyes. He could feel the thick dust crusting in the sweat on his face.

"The only white you've got left now is in your eyes," Jimmy said. "We're both Indians now. We're dust brothers!" They both laughed. "Got a handkerchief?"

"Yeah...I have." Glen remembered the large, red bandana his mother had bought for him at the beginning of the summer. It might come in handy in lots of ways, she said. He spread it across his mouth and nose and tied it tightly behind his head. He felt immediate relief from the dust.

Suddenly Glen thought of Jana. And her father.

"Hey, Lone Ranger!" Jimmy called. "What's wrong, Lone Ranger? Tonto ready to help."

"Thank you, Tonto," Glen said, as the whistle on the great steam engine in the lane announced that threshing was over for that day.

IX

The late afternoon call from the hospital came with unexpected suddenness. The doctors said it would happen within two weeks, and most everyone subconsciously interpreted that to mean at the end of two weeks. Now, it seemed unreasonable that it should have happened only three days after the doctors made the prognosis.

"Will you please carry on with the threshing, Glen?" Mrs. Hillman requested the morning after the call. "I'm counting on you now. You and Jimmy...and Enoch, of course, if you need him."

Glen stepped awkwardly from one foot to the other.

"I'm afraid I'm going to be alone for some time," she went on. "In time I expect Jana will come to terms with her father's death. She seems to be in another world at the moment, and that worries me."

The call had come from the hospital just before he came in from the threshing barn. Glen found Jana sitting at the kitchen table, crying. After a few minutes, she stopped and looked up at him. He told her he was sorry, and she cried again for a short time. She got up and almost fell into her mother's arms. Mrs. Hillman held her for quite a long time. Jana said she would like a cup of hot tea. But she didn't eat any supper. When she started for her room, her mother said goodnight to her and Jana started crying again. Then she shut the bedroom door.

"When I called her this morning she refused to get up," Mrs. Hillman continued. "I've spoken to her several times, but she doesn't answer. Do you suppose if you...?" She hesitated. "You're young, you see. If you were to speak to her.... Not a word I say is getting through to her. Am I being silly about this? I wonder if it makes any sense at all." She cupped her chin in her hand and looked at the floor.

How could he deal with something as traumatic as a father's death? He had been four years old when his own father died. Then he recalled his cousin's death.

Grief must be the same thing, no matter whether it's a father's death or a cousin's death, he thought. It's a matter of how close you were to that person. He had deeply loved his cousin, Irene. He thought she was beautiful when she came out from town to visit his family. She always treated them as being equal. She made up songs and played the new tunes on the old organ. Her curly blond hair used to bounce right along with the beat.

He was twelve when she died at eighteen.

"I'll try to help Jana," he said quickly.

Jana lay curled in a fetal position. Her face was pale and drawn, much older than her seventeen years.

"Jana!" She did not stir. "Jana! Jana!" Finally, she lifted her eyelids a little, but they closed immediately.

"I'm sorry," Glen whispered.

Mrs. Hillman put her hand on his arm and led him from the room.

"I'll have the doctor look at her just in case," she said. "I believe it is deep shock. Maybe she should be sedated."

From the kitchen window they could see Jimmy waiting for Glen, his hand on a fork handle and his eyes on the barn.

"Mr. Hillman always admired Jimmy," Mrs. Hillman commented.

"Jimmy and I will take care of things."

That night Glen stayed at Jimmy's place to make room for relatives coming to the funeral.

On the day of the funeral, Glen and Jimmy walked together to the edge of the cemetery. It would be better, Jimmy said, if they'd stay on the sidelines and not be an actual part of the funeral. Funerals were sometimes bad times for Indians. When feelings were strong, it was easier to get the Indian-white man thing going.

Jana, unaware of what was going on around

her, stood next to her mother. She made no attempt to leave the grave until her mother took her arm and led her away.

Glen closed the doors on the machinery shed. The work on the mission farm was finished for the year. It had been a good year except for Mr. Hillman's death. Mrs. Hillman would have the money she needed. Now it was time to go home.

It would be the following year before Glen would see Jana again. She'd be going back to the Academy after she was better. And he would be finishing high school. When he returned the next summer she'd be almost eighteen. They'd have lots of long conversations. They'd listen to music and....

He swung his eyes over to the woodlot. There would be walks in the woodlot.

He lifted his heavy boot over the bicycle seat, resting it on the upper pedal. Jimmy was heading down the lane for home. A foot scuffed the gravel occasionally, and his right hand slipped into his pocket to feel the small roll of bills he had earned.

X

School was out for the summer. Glen wheeled his

bicycle up to the door of the house, and slipped his arms through the straps of the big pack containing most of the clothes he owned. He had saved enough room to fit in a dozen of the Red Astrikans for Mrs. Hillman. He mounted the bicycle and turned into the lane, then stopped, and looked back at his mother and Ted standing at the door.

The early sun, still low in the eastern sky, darted through the open spaces in steady rhythm between the maples lining the road. He began to whistle a tune, timing the accents to fall on the narrow shafts of light as they flipped by him. He tried speeding up the bicycle, and speeding up the tune. He laughed to himself. That was kind of silly, wasting energy on speeding. He'd need that energy if he was going to make the twelve miles before ten o'clock.

He took several deep breaths of the delicately-scented morning air.

He thought of Jana and pressed down harder on the pedals. He wondered what he should say when he saw her.

Suddenly a small groundhog darted across the road in front of him, just missing his front wheel. He slammed on the brakes, and sat for a few moments with his eyes on the hole it dived into. Soon the small animal poked its nose up above the surface. Glen gave a short, one-note whistle, and laughed as its nose disappeared in a flash.

The morning sun began to burn down with determination and the leather straps cut at the shallow flesh above his shoulder blades. He thought of the horses he was used to seeing in the summer, their shoulders raw from the constant rubbing of the sweat-caked pads under their collars. He would be free of such scenes with the tractor doing all the pulling.

He thought of Jana again. Would she be glad to see him? He wondered.

Jana stood at the kitchen door.

"You're...you're older."

"Well, as much as I tried, I found it impossible to remain seventeen," she replied, chiding him a little. "And, I believe, let's see...oh yes, I'm sure you are older also."

"I didn't mean to say that. I wanted to say I was glad to see you and...I just wanted..." His eyes fell on hers.

"I'm glad to see you, too," she said.

She toyed with a string of opal-like beads she wore close to her throat. "Are you all right?"

"Fine." He was beginning to relax.

"Mother is waiting." She reached out and touched the back of his hand, sending a mild jolt of electricity through him. She led him through the open door into the kitchen. For a moment he forgot what he was going to say to her mother. He reached into his pack and brought out the apples.

"Astrikans!" Jana spread the apples out on the table. "You see, I did remember their name from last year. They're a little late for lunch, but tonight, perhaps. Mother loves these. She'll have them in a pie before a bat can blink an eye. After lunch we can take a walk down by the river. It will be the first time for me this year."

"Sure."

"'The song my paddle sings,'" she said, laughing a little. "Pauline Johnson, my heroine. Not in every sense of the word, but still.... Her paddle didn't always sing. There were those other times."

"Pauline Johnson was half-white, you know," he said.

"But it was her Indian blood that put the music in her paddle, I believe," she countered. "Would you agree with that?"

He didn't know what to say.

"It doesn't matter much," she said. "But lunch does."

As she walked across the kitchen, her brightly-coloured dress playfully followed the contours of her body. He wanted to run to her, to take her in his arms, to feel her firm breasts pressed against his chest as his lips came down on hers....

"Mother," Jana called. "Mother, our young gentleman has arrived."

"Glen!" Mrs. Hillman approached him with a broad smile. At first she just took his hand in hers. Then she moved closer and put one arm around his waist, pressing him toward her. "You've kept your promise."

"I didn't want any other job. I'd never find another job like this."

"We'll try to fulfil your expectations," she said. "I'm sure we'll all be very satisfied."

There were some new lines on Mrs. Hillman's face, and her eyes seemed to have lost some of the good blueness they had the previous year. Her red hair, not as rich now, was swept back from her high forehead and pinned at the back. Somehow it made her look older. The last year must have been lonely for her, he thought.

"I'm really glad to be back," he said, as they walked to the dining room.

Mrs. Hillman smiled. "I'm quite sure it will be

a good year. But Enoch will not be coming as often. We must not demand too much of him. His sensible advice will always be there if needed."

"I can handle things," Glen said. "I can take care of things myself." He caught a quick glance of satisfaction on Jana's face, but he also saw a suggestion of doubt in her soft brown eyes.

They had just seated themselves comfortably at the table, when the roar of an airplane caused them to put down their forks.

"That's the third one today." Mrs. Hillman's face grew serious. "I'm very afraid it's beginning. The rumbles coming out of Europe are frequent and ominous."

On Sunday afternoon Glen and Jana went for a walk to the river. They returned by way of the woodlot. At the edge of the clover field, they sat down to rest.

"What are you going to be?" Glen asked Jana.

"I don't know...maybe a teacher. Maybe a poet like Pauline Johnson. Maybe I'll just be a farmer," she giggled.

A yellow airplane came into view flying at low altitude.

"That's what I'd like to do," Glen said. "I'd like to fly."

"Mother says those planes belong to the Air Force and that they're practising for something."

"Maybe, but.... There he comes again. Let's wave at him."

They jumped to their feet. Glen tore off his blue shirt and swung it as high as he could. The plane dipped its wings and circled, then flew away gaining altitude quickly.

"I wish I was that guy," Glen said. "The next time a plane like that comes over here it might be me," he joked. "If something is going to happen, maybe I could be a part of it."

"Do you want to kiss me...just a little?" she asked.

He turned to her.

"It's all right," she said. "I just thought it would be fun."

He looked back at the edge of the forest where they had rested, then at her eyes again. He started to reach out to her.

"Jana!" Her mother's clear voice carried across the field and echoed against the wood-lot...*Jana...Jana...Jana....*

The words soared up and up to the top of the

trees. He was holding her firmly in his arms. He let his lips fall gently on hers as she closed her eyes. He pressed his mouth to hers and pulled her tightly to him.

"Supper!"

Jana moved away.

XI

NATIONAL REGISTRATION. The bold headlines caught the eyes of all subscribers who pulled the newspaper from their mailboxes that morning.

Jana glanced at the bold letters, then quickly took the paper to the house. "What does this mean, Mother? What is National Registration?"

Her mother dropped the mop and sat down at the table with the paper. She scanned the two-column article, then slapped the article face down on the chair beside her.

"I don't like the sound of this."

"What does it mean?"

"It means we will all be registered, every last one of us. The Federal Government will know the name, the age, the sex, the marital status, the religion, the racial origin, and the language of every soul in this country."

"What will you put down for religion?"

"I'll simply state that we have no religion."

"They'll have a hard time with the Eskimos," Jana said. "They are scattered over millions of square miles according to our geography teacher at the Academy. And they have numbers for names."

"The Eskimos won't be squeezed into this scheme. They can't be regimented like the rest of us."

"Regimented?" Jana's brow furrowed.

"The heavy hand of government is going to make itself felt." Her mother gave a wry laugh. "We're going to be recognized at last, it seems. There has been little indication that they even knew we existed for the last ten years. Our lives are going to be quite different from now on, my girl." Her face grew more serious. "We are being registered - conscripted - for one purpose only - war!"

"Glen has promised to take me canoeing on Sunday." Jana abruptly changed the subject.

XII

A chorus of bird songs rang through the clear morning air from the woodlot and the tall trees stretched in thin rows along the river banks.

Glen walked briskly from the garage, carrying a fishing rod and bait pail.

"Shall I make a picnic lunch?" Jana asked.

"Unless you like eating raw fish."

"Joker! I thought we might not conclude our voyage before noon. Raw fish! How could one even think of such a thing?"

"Some people eat raw fish. I've read about it."

"If you agree to forget the raw fish, I might be persuaded to make enough sandwiches for you, too."

"Agreed."

"After all, you will need something to supply muscle power to transport me. I shall lie back in blissful ecstasy as the caress of your paddle takes me into a world where dreams are the currency of poets, and music is the elixir of love."

"On the chance that you might not lose complete contact with the real world, I'm taking two paddles."

The canoe slid effortlessly along in the calm waters. It would be easy to let the imagination trick one into the world Jana envisioned, Glen thought. The warmth of the sun on his bare back and shoulders almost convinced him that that was the way the world should be seen on this morning.

The hours slipped away, while they both languished in the idyllic spell the river and the morning had concocted for them.

He had let her lie quietly with eyes closed, the rhythmic dip of his paddle making scarcely a sound to disturb her. Now his weary muscles told him it was time to have her join in paddling the canoe. He lifted his paddle and lightly tapped the gunwale.

"I wasn't really asleep, you know," she said, when he asked her if she'd like to help propel the 'magic swan.' "I was floating in a dream world of poetry and music, and glorious oneness with the universe." She paused. "Maybe I did touch the edge of sleep momentarily, for I must have been dreaming when our canoe seemed to be gliding over the sea, and the little ripples on your back were the waves. Does that sound crazy?"

It sounded crazy all right, but he did not want tell her that.

"Some things in our dreams are symbolic they say."

"Maybe it was something I picked up at school from the ballet, or the plays, that stimulated that sequence," she said.

"And I was there?"

"Not in full reality. You know how characters slip in and out of our dreams. Sometimes their presence is so vague you hardly know they're there. And sometimes their presence is so vivid, when you're not yet fully awake in the morning, you'd swear what they did in the dream really did happen."

He thought of some of his own vivid dreams, and he wondered if hers were of the kind he was now having quite regularly.

"Well?"

He turned around to face her. He hesitated.

She raised her eyebrows, crinkling the skin on her forehead. "Boys do have dreams, don't they?"

"I do," he replied. He nosed the canoe onto the point of a gravel spit.

"This will be a nice dry spot to have lunch," he said.

"Sir, your lunch will be served on a blanket tablecloth, the symbols on which blanket represent gifts of the Manitou."

"I'm honoured."

"It's not very private here, is it?" She looked around the bare patch of gravel.

"I was searching for a dry spot easily approachable by the canoe," he said, staring at the steep river banks.

"It will be fine." She carefully spread the colour-ful blanket over the bleached pebbles. "Surprise!" She removed two pieces of apple pie from the basket and placed them alongside the sandwiches.

"Ah, it looks delicious. If apple pie be the food of love.... Oh, no, it's music, isn't it? Somewhere in Shakespeare?"

After they finished their lunch, Glen pulled the canoe up onto the spit to check for damage.

"No place to lie and dream here," he said, glancing across the spit to the shore. "It's time to start back anyway. We could shortcut by hiding the canoe, and going back through the woodlot."

"I'll help power our swan on the return," Jana said, as he backed the canoe out into the channel. "May I be allowed to steer?"

"Sure."

They pulled the canoe up into the thick bushes, turned it upside down, and hid it from sight. They gathered up their belongings and started the climb up the steep river bank to the back of the woodlot.

"Do you need a rest?" Glen asked, when they reached the top.

"I know a better place. Can you guess?"

"I think so," Glen said, carefully spacing his

words.

They wandered along a path leading to the place where they had rested the previous year on a beautiful Sunday afternoon in early autumn.

"It was Indian summer, wasn't it?" Glen asked, when they reached the spot.

"So you do remember," she said. "It's just summer this time," she added, with a giggle. He glanced at her, trying to find meaning in her words. "Do you remember what I asked you that day?"

"Yes."

"Do you want me to repeat the question?"

He hesitated, his heart thumping against his chest wall.

"Do I have to speak my answer?" he asked. She reached out her hand to him. Her eyes rose to his. He let his arms move slowly around her waist and she came to him. His heart pounded fiercely as his lips brushed against hers. His arms tightened around her, and his mouth fell hard on her lips. For a moment he lost his balance. He stationed himself more securely and kissed her passionately, dropping his arms to the small of her back, urging the contours of her firm body to match his own. He lowered her to the dry grass, her body still tight to his. He kissed her repeatedly as she slipped the buttons through the buttonholes of her frock and brought his face to her breasts. For a few moments she held him there. Then she let his hands slip down to her hips. She unfastened the remaining buttons on her dress and invited him to her.

"I have always loved you," she said. As his body trembled, he told her that he loved her and there had been no other girl.

Later they lay close together, their faces turned to the blueness of the mid-summer sky.

"I love you," she said, softly.

"I love you, too," he whispered, his lips to her ear. She turned toward him and let her lips fall on his. They held each other for a few moments, then she removed her lips from his and lifted her hands to cup his face, her slim fingers coming to rest in sequence from front to back on his flushed cheeks.

"I shall never forget this moment," she said. He wrapped his hands around hers and hesitatingly withdrew them from his face.

"We'd better go," he said.

"Is that your cruel side you're now showing? Pulling me away from my safe haven out into the cold world?" She looked right at him, a quizzical smile matching the mischief in her eyes. He helped her to her feet, and drew her to him, putting a sharp kiss on her lips.

"Please repeat the question," he said.

They were still warm with laughter, as they stepped to the edge of the woodlot, where the field of rich, green clover stretched a quarter of a mile to the house.

Two young rabbits were nibbling the clover. There was a sudden whoosh of air above their heads, then a flash of wings as the talons of a large hawk struck a death blow to the body of the closest rabbit. In a split second the murderous act was repeated, and the other rabbit lay still.

The hawk's razor-sharp talons became a death vise as its great hooked beak tore at the small body. It proceeded to devour the rabbit, unconcerned by onlookers. Then the large predator returned to the first rabbit, lifted it into the air, and soared skyward on its five-foot wingspan.

XIII

It was National Registration Day. The newspaper ads and the "Due Notice" and "By Order" posters, pinned to telephone poles, had served their purpose. Not a soul in the county was unaware of this special day.

There was a hum in the air as people entered the halls and schools to have their names put down on the official forms.

Every individual was required to specify his or her racial origin, age, education, religion, sex, marital status, condition of health, special skills, and occupation.

"Occupation" brought a cynical smile to the faces of some. Their only occupation for several years had been a daily struggle to find enough food to stay alive. Others reasoned that it was better to have an occupation than not to have one, and they suddenly found occupations which were of the imagination.

A few people objected to supplying personal information about themselves. They wanted to know why such information was being documented. The answer they got from the interrogators was that it was a government requirement, and that they shouldn't worry.

Scattered among the crowd were some who did worry. There were things in their personal lives having to do with marriage and children, which until now had remained comfortably concealed in the quiet shadows of their own consciences.

The steady stream of people entering the halls and schools brushed shoulders with those leaving, some holding registration cards for all to see. There were smiling faces, but others showed signs of growing concern. They had begun to analyze the situation and had found something ominous about it.

Some of those holding up cards had not fully qualified as valued members of society. Now they had gained a kind of equality with the rest. And even if it wouldn't change their lives much, the registration was confirmation that they were a recognized part of society.

Only a few days after the registration, the headline in the morning newspapers contained one word: WAR. The five-inch black letters shouted up from the page, drowning out all about them.

The purpose of the registration was no longer a mystery.

Ads began appearing in newspapers, encouraging young men to "join up" in the military services. Farm magazines told of the need for greater production of food. The numbers of men riding on the tops of freight trains began to dwindle, and those freight trains began to carry large wooden crates and strange-looking caterpillar-tracked vehicles.

Soon, people were being re-introduced to the feel of dollar bills in pockets, which had been empty for ten years. And the term "War. Production" became an indispensable part of common vocabulary, for it was war production that was suddenly generating an economic revolution.

The money to power that revolution appeared in staggering amounts. And no one questioned how the money became available, for it brought improvement to the lives of the people and to their communities.

Some of those who were offered jobs in the cities required housing. That housing sprang up where needed, financed by a government which miraculously found the necessary dollars.

Pool rooms, previously the only recreational haunts affordable to men with few coins, now resonated to the rattle of plentiful coins in those men's pockets as they vociferously debated whether war caused depressions or ended depressions.

Colourful posters, depicting healthy-looking soldiers, sailors and airmen, found places on buildings, telephone poles and billboards. Some posters had fingers pointing out to the public with the message: Your Country Needs You. And some showed men climbing into airplanes or on ships at sea, or manning tanks and guns. In all cases the men were in clean uniforms in clean environments.

For men who had been deprived of basic necessities, living lacklustre lives, the posters portrayed a glorious adventure in which their lives would attain a degree of satisfaction and importance.

Newspapers constantly carried ads for government. Soon it was difficult to find a paper critical of any aspect of government policy. The national radio became a propaganda tool for government. Soon, any questioning of Canada's role in the war was considered tantamount to treason.

It was easy to be swept up in the tide of patriotic fervour as it was propelled by an incessant stream of propaganda.

The word propaganda, once a legitimate word, had become a "bad" word as a result of propaganda's having become a notorious tool put to use by the enemy. But the connotation of the word did not preclude its practical application by the allied nations.

Some papers exhorted people to hate the enemy, then forgive him if they could find it in their hearts to do so. Old words such as Hun were dredged up to vilify the enemy. It didn't matter if the application of the word, in the modern context, was incorrect. Its historical connotation made it an effective propaganda weapon.

In a matter of a few weeks, most elements of society were caught up in the fervour in an all-out effort to save the mother country. People of English blood often found themselves pushed to the fore-front, their status suddenly elevated. And some found it difficult to resist acting in accordance with the status their heritage afforded them.

Many of the British instructors who came to Canada lorded it over the "colonials." It was of little consequence that the young men were putting their lives on the line for the mother country; they were still colonials to the instructors.

It was inevitable, with the severe losses on the war front, that Canada would be called upon to make a greater contribution. The Prime Minister's "not nec-essarily conscription, but conscription if necessary," would have to find an interpretation justifying con-scription. In the plebiscite which followed, the peo-ple, caught up in the tide of patriotism, brought in a majority vote for conscription. What little opposi-tion there was was quashed.

As heavy casualties continued to mount up, the government found it necessary to pass legislation permitting married men, with or without children, to be conscripted for military service.

Some essential workers were exempted from conscription, as were divinity students.

"Thou shalt not kill" was absent from sermons, as the seminarians thanked God for victories in which thousands of young men and women on both sides were killed.

Some seminarians also secretly thanked God for their exemptions. But there were those seminarians who did go out of patriotism and there were those who went because it was important that God be kept on the side of the forces allied against the Axis powers.

Patriotic Societies were formed to present young men and women with wristwatches and to bid them farewell. At such gatherings, noted speakers, much beyond conscription age, talked of the glory of serving one's country and of the quality of men and women who were prepared to put themselves in mortal danger for such purpose.

Some young men seemed surprised at the sudden importance attributed to them, especially by speakers who until then had ignored their existence. Still, the public accepted such praise for their young men and women, even if the words of some speakers were more political than patriotic.

As *There'll Always be an England* rang out at social gatherings and in dance halls, young men of conscription age moved closer to girlfriends. And some established new friendships to fulfil some deep need they held within themselves.

Quick marriages were arranged, some through necessity. Such marriages, normally frowned upon, were acceptable in view of the unusual circumstances.

There were also marriages because men subconsciously thought they would be more likely to come back home if they had something to come back to. Coupled with this was the instinctive need to produce offspring, and something told them that a child would be a bond holding their small family together although they would be far apart.

In the clean, quiet Sunday morning, people sat less comfortably in the pews and listened to their leaders give thanks for victories which cost the lives of Canadian servicemen.

There were few who were able to maintain their original enthusiasm for the war effort as casualty lists rattled the telegraph keys with greater frequency.

Parents were much concerned for their children who were nearing conscription age. And some parents suffered the condemnation of the majority when they questioned sending their sons off to fight in foreign lands. Derogatory terms such as "Zombie" were applied to young men who did not willingly join the services. Those men were conscripted, and sent to guard war prisoners, and to administer the internment camps containing Canadians of several ethnic groups the government thought dangerous.

Many of the internees were first-class Canadians. Some of them had established businesses. Those businesses were confiscated and became the property of the Federal Government. The cruel and unconstitutional measures taken by government were accepted as necessary, for "Nothing matters now but victory" was the clarion call. Nothing actual or imagined would be allowed to stand in the way.

XIV

Jimmy Sondol had no intention of staying away from the war.

"I'm going!" he called out as he approached Glen on his bicycle. "See this. It's a notice to get a medical examination. I've never had one in my life.

It doesn't cost anything."

"The army?" Glen asked.

"Yeah. I don't have to go like the white guys, but I'm going. It's my chance to amount to some-thing. If I miss it, I might never get another chance. They say they train you in lots of things."

"Did you go down to the hall when the recruit-ing officer was there?" Glen asked.

"Yeah. When I told him I could kill a rabbit at three hundred yards he said I was the kind they needed."

"Jimmy, did he tell you you'd be killing men?"

"That's the part I don't like, but I guess I might do it if I had to." Jimmy looked down at the ground, then away to the horizon, his ear tuned to the drone of an airplane. "What about you?"

"That's what I'd like," Glen said. "To be in an airplane. I'd like to fly an airplane," he added, as the plane came toward them at high speed, skipping the tree tops. "I never saw one with two engines."

"It's a bomber," Jimmy informed him. "The recruiting officer had a picture he showed some guys standing around the counter. He said they might get a chance to fly a plane like that...even a four-engine bomber.

"I got to go," he said, his voice impatient, his

foot poised on the pedal. "I want to be there early, before the other guys."

"Glen," Mrs. Hillman called from the door, "Would you ride down to Enoch's place and ask him if he'll take charge when the two heifers freshen in October? It will be nice to have our own milk again."

"October?"

Mrs. Hillman watched as he slowly recovered the bicycle from the shed. He mounted it, sitting still for a few moments before heading out the lane.

"Glen seems worried," Mrs. Hillman remarked to Jana. "Is there something bothering him?"

"Oh, I don't think I'm a bother," Jana said, half joking. "It's more likely the war, don't you think? His school friends are all joining the services."

"Has he said what his plans are?"

"He's talked about the Air Force. I'm not sure how serious he is. He said he'll have to decide when his conscription notice arrives."

"This hellish war! One would think that reason might prevail after the last war. Sometimes I think the human species is hell-bent on its own destruction.

"And you?" She looked at Jana. "Where do you stand in all of this? Have you discussed your future?"

"Some."

"Some? What kind of an answer is that? Is that all you have to say? Don't you understand the seriousness of this war? You had better think about it. What's your association with him?"

"Oh, Mother, I...I wish you'd leave that to me."

"Sure. Leave it to you. Leave it to you when all those silly girls your age are running away and getting married to boys they'll never see again. And what for? Tell me that!"

"Mother..." The words stuck in her throat. Her mother's arms flew out to encircle her, as they had so many times when she was growing up, those arms that seemed to always be there when she needed them.

"I love him," Jana said.

Her mother didn't say anything right away, but she stood back and folded her arms in that determined stance of hers.

"Things will be all right, my girl," her mother sighed.

When Glen neared Enoch's place, he called out his usual greeting in the Delaware language Enoch had taught him. It meant: "I share the wonder of life with you this day."

But Enoch did not appear at the door in his clean overalls, his hands held open to receive Glen as a trusted friend. And Enoch was not in the garden, where his "honest relationship with nature" had resulted in an abundance of fruit and vegetables, now maturing in the mellowness of early September.

"He's not there," a voice called from the road. "He's down at the monument."

Glen looked up to see Bertrand, squatted on a broken-down bike, casting an envious glance at his bicycle.

"Monument?"

"You know, that tall thing where the names are cut into the stone. I can't think of the name of it."

"The cenotaph?"

"Yeah, that's it."

"Thanks." Bertrand didn't seem threatening this morning. He gave the impression he would like to talk if Glen had the time, but Glen started to pedal away.

"I might go to the war," Bertrand called after him. "The man from Ottawa said we're all brothers in a war."

Glen wasn't so sure he was ready to be a brother with Bertrand just yet. But he thought

about the word *brother* as he rode toward the cenotaph. It was true, as Bertrand suggested, that they
were all brothers in war. One could not honestly
think of it otherwise, not when they were all lined
up facing the enemy together.

Enoch stood perfectly still, his eyes fixed on the
names carved into the stone column. He was saying
something in a quiet monotone. Glen strained his
ears to catch the words, but they were in the
Delaware language. Finally Enoch turned and
walked toward him.

"I share the sorrow of the day with you," he
said, his kind face placid. "I share the glory of life
with you this day." Enoch turned back to the cenotaph. "They are my brothers," he said. "We were
only boys. I promised their spirits I would share my
life with them. It has been many years...many seasons. On this morning, when the good earth glories
in the abundance of living things, I think of the lives
of young men. My heart remembers the lives stolen
from young men by the generals. We were sent to
tear other young men apart like wild dogs."

Glen tried not to show his embarrassment. He
didn't think Enoch believed in spirits, at least not to
the extent revealed in his words. It seemed so alien,

even silly. He had never been able to penetrate completely the minds of the Indians, even Enoch's, although he was so clear about most things.

"We must not forget the beauty and glory of life, even when the destruction of war has made our eyes blind to that beauty." His grey eyes searched Glen's face and turned back to the cenotaph.

"The wild dogs have been turned loose again," he said.

Glen pushed his bicycle as they walked slowly back to Enoch's place.

"We bend music to suit our purpose," Enoch said suddenly. "The war makes use of good music. Music that uplifts the human spirit, but is used in killing. Is it a denial of the truth? Maybe only the generals can answer that." There was a rare cynical note to his voice.

For a moment Glen worried that Enoch was back at the cenotaph. Then Enoch said he looked forward to Mrs. Hillman's next musical evening. On that evening, they'd celebrate the birth of two new calves, and the goodness of the new milk.

Glen's conscription notice arrived on schedule. It was a time when all government documents took priority, and the post office was quick to determine the addresses of young men working away from home.

The muffled hum of voices carried into the elevator when it came to a stop at the second floor of the large office building. As the door opened, Glen was confronted by a wave of young men noisily pursuing their way to various cubicles.

"Aircrew to the right; ground crew to the left," the middle-aged sergeant kept calling at intervals. Young men from farms, towns and cities mingled together, their excitement registered in the rising pitch of their voices.

Glen held back until some noisy braggarts were assigned cubicles appropriate to the educational skills their documents confirmed. He approached the long counter and laid his high school diploma and birth certificate before a neatly-dressed officer. The officer perused the documents quickly.

"Your name?"

"It's on the documents, sir."

"I want to hear it from you," the officer stated. "We have to make sure the documents fit the man. Now, your name, quickly!"

"My name is Glen Hansen."

"I believe everything is in order," the officer

remarked, after a few minutes. "Education, Medical Certificate, Proof of Birth. I assume you are hoping to be aircrew."

"Yes, I'd like to be a pilot."

"Why?" The officer stared at him.

"I...I think it would be exciting."

"Do you think it would be exciting to drop bombs on people who are in the way of targets?"

"No, but if that's what happens..." He could not continue. Drop bombs on people? Kill them? He swallowed hard.

"We like to see the reaction when the seriousness of this business is brought home to young men who think this is going to be a lark. If you had reacted with a laugh, I would have grounded you at the start. It may seem strange, but we know that a man without a conscience has no place in an airplane loaded with bombs. And if you're wondering, be assured that I am speaking from experience. Go to section A. The interrogator will determine the stream to which you will be assigned."

As Glen stood by the highway, hitch-hiking a ride home, he began to feel the excitement of being part of the aircrew. He would be a flight engineer, they told him. He was the kind of young man they needed.

For the moment, any thought of killing people seemed far distant. He could see himself taking responsibility for the plane's engines and controls as he talked back and forth on the intercom with the pilot. They would be flying through a blue sky filled with puffy, white clouds, high above the ocean, which seemed to stretch out forever before them.

The beeping of a musical horn jolted him. He looked up to see a black Buick stopped a short distance ahead. He stepped quickly to the passenger side of the car and eased the door open.

"I'm not quite sure about offering you a ride," the middle-aged lady stated. "But I guess you are all right."

"I assure you I am."

"Well then, if you'll arrange yourself, we'll be on our way." She smiled and pulled the car out onto the highway.

She was slightly intimidating in her fine dress and expensive jewellery. He had never been that close to a lady quite like her. She'd be about fifty, he thought. Her slightly-greying hair was swept back from her forehead, and her expressive hazel eyes looked through fancy-rimmed glasses connected to her collar by a black cord. Her thin fingers were adorned by two gold rings, one with a glittering diamond.

Her hands rested comfortably on the steering wheel as she guided the car along at forty miles an hour, the speed limit imposed to conserve scarce gasoline.

"I'm from New York," she said. "I suppose you noticed my license plates."

"No," he said. "I guess I was thinking about airplanes."

"Are you a service man?"

"Not yet, but I will be soon."

She frowned. "So many young men. Girls too.... Many of them to be sacrificed in this insane war plaguing the world. It's such a contradiction to the life I have enjoyed." She looked at him. "My life has been in the Arts, more precisely in music: operas and operettas. Do you like music?"

"Yes I...I don't know much about music." He thought of Jana. He could still see her on that musical evening, the warm light of the hanging lamp falling softly on her face and silhouetting her beautiful form. He wanted to go to her and put his arms around her and draw her to him.

"My name is Cory," she said. "My married name is Goeppeles. I'm on my way to London to visit my elderly mother. In these troubled times, family seems to be very important." She glanced over at him again.

"I'm so glad I had the courage to offer you a ride," she went on. "It's much more pleasant riding with someone. It helps one to maintain a kind of reality. You see, most of my life has been in the unreal world, the world of the imagination. It's easy to fall back into that world when one is seeking refuge." She reached to turn on the radio. "Perhaps we can find some nice music. Music is in the real world, and in the world of the imagination. That's the nice thing about it."

She sounded a little like Jana, Glen thought. Jana! If the message telling him to report came on the weekend, he might never see her again! For a moment he felt as though he had been punched in the guts. Then he got hold of himself. The recruiting officer had said there wasn't much chance the notice would arrive that soon.

The radio was blaring out a song about airmen coming back from a night-bombing run with the plane shot up and one engine gone. But they had *hit their target*, and it had been a *great show* and a *great sight*.

Mrs. Goeppeles took a deep breath. "So much

of the music is geared to war now. I find it difficult to accommodate some of the material spewing out from radios and spread across the news pages." She snapped off the radio. "I believe for the balance of our short odyssey I would prefer good conversation."

When Glen got to the mission farm Enoch was there about the heifers, and Jana was picking gladiolus in the garden.

Jana stood up when she sensed his presence. She turned quickly toward him, her light frock swinging after her, and wrapping itself around her legs, then falling back. The brilliant gladiolus resting against her breast reflected soft pastels on her light brown skin.

"I'm going," he said, forgetting all the words he had so carefully prepared. She stood motionless for an instant, then stepped slowly toward him. Finally, she took one long step and fell into his arms.

"I had a terrible feeling I might never see you again," he said. "I know it's silly, but that's what happened. It's crazy, isn't it?"

"No," Jana replied. "If it's crazy, then I'm crazy too. Mother and I both harboured that terrible thought. We knew there wasn't any justification for it, still, it was there." She took a deep breath, and he let her back from him.

"You know something? I haven't even kissed you," he said. "All the way over here I was going to kiss you every time I told you something new about what happened."

"Do you wish to start?" she asked, puckering her lips, as she stretched to reach him. They ducked behind a row of young spruces, and there, wrapped in the perfume of white clover, their love was consummated.

Mrs. Hillman was sitting on the bench by the lilac tree, bidding Enoch goodbye, when Jana and Glen came around the house to the kitchen door. Their flushed faces would be normal by the time Mrs. Hillman walked back from the road, they thought. They were safe.

XV

One day before the calves were to be born, Glen's younger brother wheeled past the lilac tree up the lane to the house. In his basket was a brown envelope carrying the stamp of The Department of National Defence.

Glen's nervous fingers tore open the envelope and unfolded the stiff sheet of paper it contained. NOTICE TO REPORT. He was to report to Manning Pool in Toronto November 1. His future had been laid out for him in painfully clear words.

November! It would be much easier to obey the order in the warmth of July, Glen thought.

"Mother said if they're going to get you soon you should come home and spend the last days," Ted stated. "And you could help with the late apples, too."

"I'll come back before I have to go," Glen told him. "I'll soon be through here." But he knew he would never be through at the mission farm while Jana was part of it. "Tell Mother I'll find some way to work things out."

"I'll tell her," Ted said, lifting a sack of apples from his pack. "She sent these." He turned his bicycle around and started down the lane. "I wish you'd come back," he called over his shoulder. Glen waved and watched him turn onto the road toward the bridge.

He had not been a very good brother to Ted in the last three or four years. He saw the effects in Ted's eyes when he lifted the apples over the handle bars.

In three years Ted would be eligible for con-scription. Maybe the war would be over by then. If it wasn't, his mother would be left alone when they took Ted.

He had thought of mentioning Jana to Ted, but maybe Ted would think of that as a lame excuse for not coming home. There must be some way for him to accommodate both his needs and those of his family. Maybe Jana could help him find a way.

Glen placed the sack of apples on the table by the window. "I haven't much time left," he said.

"But you do have time for apple pie, do you not?" Mrs. Hillman asked.

The kitchen normally had a warm atmosphere when Mrs. Hillman was in it. She knew how to say things in a way that made sense and still allowed for humour and the expression of satisfaction she found in life.

"Jana, see if we have some good cheese left. 'Apple pie without the cheese...is like a kiss without the squeeze,'" she quoted. The words brought an immediate end to any suggestion of gloom.

Jana giggled and handed the block of cheese to her mother.

"What a delightful rhyme," she remarked. "Apples, cheese, kisses, squeeze. Now I'll have to exchange music for apples and cheese as the food of love. It's better anyway, don't you think?"

"But squeeze should be squeezes," Glen protested. "All the other words are plural."

"Ah," Jana responded, "A singular squeeze will satisfy many kisses. Argue with that fact," she challenged, tapping her fingers on the sack of apples for emphasis.

"Silly girl," Mrs. Hillman chided. "We all seem to be acting like children. Pick out a half dozen apples and start peeling them. Now that would be silly if I said it, wouldn't it? If I said you were the apple of my eye? Maybe you both are the apple of my eye," she mused.

"Apples, Mother, in the plural," Jana corrected.

"My, but we are literary this morning," Mrs. Hillman remarked.

XVI

The birth of the calves came on schedule.

It was a welcome change to have some positive things to help balance the negative news from the battlefronts. One positive thing was the bountiful supply of milk. Now there would be cream and butter to enrich a diet depleted by rationing.

Jana looked up from the butter bowl and glanced at the reds and yellows still clinging to the maples at the edge of the woodlot. She put the butter ladle down, and stared out the window.

The woodlot seemed to be moving away from her as the Indian summer haze vibrated its margins in slow harmonic waves. She let her eyes follow the mildly hypnotic action, and soon she was swaying rhythmically. Her heart began to beat against her chest wall, and her short breaths fell into time with her gyrating body.

She and Glen had lain in the secret nest three times in the last days before he left. Little was said of the future.

On the last day, Glen's nervousness would not let him remain silent for long.

"I want to marry you," he said, "before I go."

"But you are leaving tomorrow," she reminded him.

"I mean before I go overseas."

"Now that makes more sense."

"Do you want me to repeat the question?" he asked.

"But there was no question," she said, ready to play his game.

"Then what did I say?"

"It seems to me, that in dealing with a subject of such magnitude, and in view of the serious implications, one might reasonably expect that words would be carefully chosen."

"I was so damned excited I could have said anything!" he blurted out. "I wanted to ask you a long time ago but I knew I couldn't." Her warm hand slid slowly over his face, her fingers coming to rest in consecutive order from his cheek to his ear lobe.

"Do you wish to question the plaintiff?"

"I do, Your Honour."

"Proceed."

"Your Honour, I wish to tell the plaintiff that I want to marry her."

"Don't tell me what you want to say to the plaintiff. Tell her directly."

Glen raised himself on his elbow. Looking straight into her moist eyes, he asked in a controlled tone: "Will you marry me?"

She lifted herself up and put her lips to his ear. "Yes," she whispered. He took her in his arms and they fell back on the soft bed of dry grass.

"I never dreamed that question could knock one out like a punch in the guts," he said, as he lay limp.

"There is a treatment for emotional exhaustion," she stated. She let her lips slide down to his in a lingering kiss.

"Jana!" Her mother's voice startled her into the reality of the present. "I thought you were going to tumble over. Are you all right?"

"I think so, Mother, as right as it is possible to be..." Glen had been gone three days. She was already missing him desperately. Was this the way it was going to be? she wondered, as she sat down for a cup of tea with her mother.

That night at supper she did not eat anything. Even the baked potatoes smothered in fresh butter failed to kindle her interest in food.

She began to worry about the application she had submitted to the London Teachers College. In her present state, she would never be able to face interrogation by the professors. She would have to find a way to get hold of herself, and soon.

She knew she would need a discipline which dealt with a completely new area of life. She wasn't sure where to look for that kind of discipline. But maybe, if she set her heart to it, there would still be time to find it. And perhaps by the date of her appointment at the College, she would have adapted sufficiently to live in that changed world which now was hers.

XVII

"This is the day. Have you forgotten?" Mrs. Hillman reached for her basket. "Now that you and Glen have made plans, it's only proper that you meet his mother without delay. I'm a little worried about the blood."

"Blood?"

"Indian blood. Have you forgotten your Indian blood?"

"Certainly not."

"Neither have many of the people living beyond the reserve."

There was something strangely ominous about her mother's words.

"I don't wish to alarm you, my girl, but reality is reality, and you had better take that into account and prepare for it. And no matter that you are a beautiful and talented girl, it's 'Indian' the white people see first. Some, I believe, get to the place where they see very little Indian, and they begin to value the qualities which make that Indian person what he is."

"Or what she is?"

"I suppose I was thinking of your father when I put it that way," her mother replied.

She thought back to the day she first saw Roy. He and Mr. Vogler were clearing the mission farm of the scrub trees which took over the land once the Moravians were gone. She was doing research for an essay on Tecumseh. Someone told her that Mr. Vogler was part Delaware Indian. He could supply all the information she would need on Tecumseh. And he could tell her about the settlement where the Moravians taught the Indians about agriculture, as well as religion.

Her essay had become a major project and required several visits to the farm and the old cemetery where the Moravians were buried. It was on the second trip to the river cemetery that she began to see the boy as something other than Indian when she looked at his quiet, intelligent face.

The chief of The Delaware Indian Band had said he would like to read her essay some time. Some people weren't very accurate in stories about the Indians, he said. When she took the essay to him the following summer, she went to visit Roy and Mr. Vogler, who were still clearing the mission farmland. When she and Roy were walking back from the field to the road, she stopped and let her eyes scan the land stretching back to the river.

"I think this would be a lovely place to live," she said.

Roy smiled.

"Maybe I will come back and live here," she said, half joking.

"I wish you would, Katherine," Roy said.

She knew at that moment, that when she finished her university degree, she would find her way back to the mission farm.

"Mother?"

"I believe I was letting myself slip away for a moment," her mother confessed. The warm smile that so often welcomed her as a child returned to her mother's face for a moment, then dissolved in a mildly serious expression.

Jana looked closely at her. Her mother was getting older; there was no doubt about that. Her handsome red hair was gradually losing its brilliance, and her eyes, while still intelligent, had lost some of the "flash of fire in the wigwam." Glen's mother would get old, too. Now Jana's apprehension gave way to the excitement she felt in meeting her for the first time.

It had been more than five years since the July day when they turned into the lane and observed two boys working at the edge of the orchard. The tart red apples they bargained for led to the conversation resulting in Glen's employment at the mission farm. "Indian" - that's how Glen had seen her. He had looked at her in quick glances, then at her mother. Otherwise he showed no interest in her.

Maybe Glen had said enough about her to soften the Indian part. Maybe along with the Indian part his mother would be searching for other things about her. She would try to show the qualities she possessed. She could make use of the discipline she learned in ballet classes. Her speech would match her sophisticated poise. She would present that striking pose her ballet instructor referred to on several occasions.

Jana got out of the car and quickly smoothed her bright flowered frock. A badly weathered door, set in a crooked frame, stood open to a dirt yard surrounding the aged frame house. Jana reached for her mother's hand as they moved to within a few feet of the door.

"She's around at the back doing the washing," a voice called from a distance. They stopped abruptly and turned to see Ted carrying a container of apples toward a long row of apple crates.

"Go on around," Ted said when they hesitated. He sounded resentful, Jana thought. They had taken Glen away from him, and from his mother. That's how Ted's young mind seemed to interpret it. She felt a slight tinge of guilt. She would try to make it up to Ted. They could buy some apples from him. That would be a start. But now she needed all her concentration in negotiating with his mother.

"Good morning, Mrs. Hansen." Mrs. Hillman's greeting seemed to surprise Glen's mother, and she dropped the heavy overalls she was hand-wringing back into the tub.

"How do you do," she answered, smoothing her dress over her hips with her wet hands.

"I'm Mrs. Hillman, and this is my daughter Jana."

"How do you do," Mrs. Hansen said, without betraying any discernible emotion. She glanced at her knuckles, raw from the washboard. "I must apologize for my appearance," she explained. "Washday is a rather ragged day."

"Please don't apologize. It is we who should apologize, dropping in on you with so little notice." Mrs. Hansen looked surprised.

"Notice?" she questioned. Mrs. Hillman turned to Jana.

"Did you ask Glen to convey the message to Mrs. Hansen that we would like to visit her today?"

"Yes," Jana answered. "He said he'd deliver the message." She felt Mrs. Hansen's strong eyes focus on her. "I'm terribly sorry, Mrs. Hansen. It's a dreadful intrusion on your privacy. There has to be an explanation." As she spoke Ted approached carrying a bushel of apples. He stopped a few feet from them and put down the basket.

"Is something wrong?"

"Ted, did Glen say anything about visitors today?"

"Yeah," Ted answered. "He told me at the railroad station, when he said to give them a bushel of the best apples. I thought you knew all about it."

"It seems I'm the only one who didn't know all about it."

"Perhaps in his preoccupation it slipped Glen's mind completely," Mrs. Hillman suggested.

"Yes, he seemed very occupied...about a lot of things." Mrs. Hansen's eyes swung up to Jana. This time there was a suggestion of understanding in those eyes, even kindness. She turned slowly and looked over to the far side of the orchard.

She was helping to pick the northern spys on that early November day. The labour pains came on so suddenly and severely her husband had to carry her to the house. He laid her on the bed, then ran across the field to the neighbours to telephone the doctor. When he returned, she presented him with a baby boy. He almost fainted when she made him cut the cord. Now that son was being taken from her - a son she might never set eyes on again after he left for overseas.

This girl who stood before her would be allied with her. They would have to find a way to share their love for Glen and for each other. It would take love to deal with what the future held for both of them. It would be good to have this girl as an ally; this girl Glen said was beautiful and talented, and part-Indian.

"Ted, take Mrs. Hillman and Jana over to that nice bench by the greening tree. I'll make some tea to go with the apple fritters. It'll be no time with that roaring fire I've got going to heat the wash water."

The smell of fresh apples filled the air around them as Jana and Mrs. Hillman drove home. Along the quiet roads Indian summer lingered in the fading colours of the maples and sumach.

"She's a woman to be reckoned with," Mrs. Hillman remarked.

"Do you think so, Mother? Do you think we'll get along all right?"

"Yes, my girl, I do. She's a perceptive woman. Did you notice that?"

"I thought those eyes were scrutinizing me quite painstakingly."

"If it were your son, would you be any less scrutinizing?"

"Mother, please let's not leap too far into the future. I'm not even married yet, you know."

XVIII

Glen stepped off the train in Regina with two hundred other young men, all of whom would now be known as airmen. They were loaded into trucks covered with tarpaulins and whisked away in the direction of an air base designated a Service Flying Training School.

The tall elevators rose up from the prairie in vivid contrast to the flat spaces beyond.

There was enough room to swallow the world if

need be - certainly the world of small spaces, comfortably interspersed with trees and streams that Glen knew. How could anyone ever feel secure in the vast openness of the unsheltered prairie? he wondered.

He would have to adjust, as would the young men around him, many of whom were silently trying to accommodate the vast dimensions of the land spreading out before them.

And they would all have to get used to the crude remarks of some loud-mouthed, non-commissioned officers who seemed more interested in intimidation than instruction.

"I'll say what I have to say only once!" the sergeant barked, as they were lined up on the railroad platform and told to identify themselves by name and number.

"You're not dealing with your favourite auntie now," he said in an abrasive voice. "You'll be told when to eat, when to go to bed, when to get up, and what to do every hour of the day and night, except when you're snuggled down in those luxury bunks, which, by the way, you'll keep perfectly made up, or you'll end up peeling potatoes and cleaning latrines." A sadistic smile pushed up the corners of his moustache as he waited for the slightest indication of protest.

"We're in a deadly serious game. We have one purpose only, and that is to make you part of the great killing machine being built to obliterate a vicious enemy before they can take over the world." He waited for his words to sink in, observing the shock registered on some of the young faces.

"This isn't Sunday School," he said. "You damn well better remember that!"

The occasional blocks of beige grassland, spotted among the patchwork of wheat stubble and fallow land, looked mellow in the late autumn sun. But there was something forbidding about it. It didn't invite you to go and lie down in it, the way the warm grass at home did.

"What do you think?" a sturdy-looking boy asked.

"It's big, isn't it, almost too big for your eyes to take in."

"Not for me," the young man said. "I was born on the prairies, a few miles from here. Do you like it?"

"I'm not sure yet. Maybe I could like it, if I set my mind to it," Glen replied.

"You had better take a good look. Any day now the whole thing will be covered with snow, and when it gets thirty or forty below, that snow locks onto the ground until April, even May sometimes. Then spring comes all at once, and you forget that the snow has locked you in for six months."

"It must be hard to survive such a climate."

"We're pretty tough out here. Maybe that's why the prairie guys make good sailors. They always have to think of survival. Do you know what I mean?"

"I think so," Glen replied.

"They say the prairie people are good at just about anything. I guess it's partly true."

Glen took a closer look at the boy. The prairie had helped make him what he was, he said. He would be a survivor. You could see it in his face.

"What's your name?" Glen asked.

"Kramer," he answered, "Ed Kramer."

"My name is Hansen, Glen Hansen."

Ed's eyes swept over the broad expanse of prairie he said would soon be covered with snow.

"You know what I'm going to miss most of all?" Ed asked. "The library, that's what." He proceeded to tell how, on their weekly visits to town on Saturdays, he'd load up with library books. There was nothing else to do on the long winter nights but read. It was easier after they got the hydro. There were no hydro lines before they built the air base.

"I figure I've learned a fair amount about this country from reading. I've read about its forests, its great rivers, its lakes, its mining, its history, exploration, and the men who pioneered flying in the north - Dickens and Wop May and guys like that. They had rickety old single-engine planes. Not like the twins we're going to fly.

"I learned quite a bit about politics from reading, but I could never understand politicians." He paused and looked out at the prairie again. "We damn near starved for four bad years, and there wasn't a nickel in our pockets. All of a sudden the politicians found lots of money. I've wondered where the money came from to get our air base built in such a hurry."

In the distance, a yellow speck, accelerating down a black ribbon of asphalt, became an airplane which vaulted into the air and streaked toward them. Glen felt his heart skip a beat. He'd soon be in a plane like that. He wondered what it would feel like.

"We might be gone by the time spring comes," Ed remarked. Again he shifted his eyes to scan the broad land.

The impact of his statement struck Glen sharply. By spring, he could be overseas with the rest of them.

He would have a few days' leave at Christmas. That time would be divided equally between his home and the mission farm.

Before they went overseas, the men said, there would be something called departure leave.

The roar of a plane's engines overhead reminded him that in a few hours he'd be getting down to serious training. He was ready to start.

XIX

Jana sat at her desk with her books pushed aside, reading the latest letter from Glen.

His first letters had been filled with the excitement of flying in the twin-engine planes.

Those who went up with him and were air sick were kept under observation. If they didn't overcome their air sickness after being up a few times they were washed out, he said.

Now his letters dealt with the serious realities of flying: the frigid weather, getting caught in icing conditions and sometimes trying to land in almost zero visibility.

Some planes on cross-country flights never came back, especially some of those on night flights. Some would be stranded on the American side of the border. Some would be found in a bundle of rubble, or in a pile of charred remains. The romance of flying had taken on a different connotation, he said.

All of Glen's letters spoke of his love for her, and his anticipation of their wedding as soon as he was allowed leave.

It was obvious that most of his time was being taken up in training. If his weekly letter was a day late, she tried to understand. She found it difficult to get a letter off to him sometimes, now that the studies at the London Teachers College demanded so much of her time. But one night when she sat thinking about why Glen's letters might be late, she began to visualize him in the arms of another girl. There were lots of girls from the city who came out to the dances on the base, he said. What did he do at the dances? Just stand around watching? Not likely!

She began to wish she had never taught him to waltz and to do the polka. It was the polka that got his blood racing, he said. And those long, graceful waltz steps she insisted on.... He'd likely be the best waltzer there. All the girls would want to dance with him. And there'd be one who would trick him into a relationship by getting him to teach her to dance. She might even trick him into marriage. Well, Jana would stop that before it got started!

The next evening, in an act of rash behaviour, she threw Glen's letters into the wastepaper basket, then quickly reached for them. She swept her books to the back of her desk and jumped up from the chair. She'd find out the truth for herself. She'd go out there; she'd leave this instant! She packed a small bag, and was about to head for the railway station when the phone rang.

"Jana?"

"Mother, what is it?"

"It's a telegram from Glen. Mrs. Southwell read it over the phone to me. There's a problem getting leave time for your wedding during the holidays. The message said not to worry, he'd try to sort things out."

When there was no response, Mrs. Hillman went on, "Jana, we'll just have to rearrange things. These situations occur frequently now."

Jana began to sob.

"Mother, I knew he'd never come back. Now

it's happened. I'm going out there!"

"You silly girl, you've let yourself get into such a state you can't keep a rational perspective on the situation. I've been sensing the change in you for some time. Now, I want you to listen, and listen carefully!

"If you indulge in foolish reactions, you may lose the most precious thing that life can offer. And for what reason? Because you have doubts about the fidelity of Glen, that most wonderful element in your life.

"And now I must tell you something. I have received two letters recently from Glen in which he expressed concern about your feelings for him. He asked me to determine how you really feel about him, what with him going overseas and all.

"Apparently two fellows in his class were promised marriage, and then the girls skipped out. The effects on those two men were disastrous. One took his own life.

"Glen asked me to keep the matter confidential. Now I have betrayed that confidentiality. Are you listening to me?"

"Yes, Mother, but I'm not sure I want to hear anything further."

"You silly girl, listen to me! There has never

been a bride-to-be in history who has not been worried sick until the moment she feels that ring pushed snugly on her nervous finger. I myself suffered the same doubts to a degree, although there were no indications of anything going wrong. Things turned out to be just the way we planned. And they will turn out for you and Glen. He assured me of his love and devotion. Did you hear that? Love and devotion!

"Plans have to be changed every day in these critical times. And people's lives simply must adjust to the changing conditions.

"Some people's lives are being destroyed today, through no fault of their own; some are being destroyed through lack of discipline." The line was quiet for some time. "I don't believe I have anything more to say."

Jana dropped the bag on her bed, and pushed the dresser drawer closed. She sat quietly on the bed for a moment, letting her mother's words ring in her head. She had been the silly girl her mother termed her.

It was only two days before a second telegram arrived saying the problem with leave had been resolved. A letter would follow.

Jana watched every morning for the delivery girl who stuffed the letters in the students' boxes at ten.

Finally, on the Monday morning after a week of anxious waiting, Jana could wait no longer. She knew the mail arrived at the farm at eleven. She picked up the phone.

"Is there any mail?" she demanded, without greeting her mother with the normal "Good Morning."

Saying "Good Morning" had been a part of the discipline of growing up, just as the "Good Afternoon" was a part of the discipline required by her ballet teacher.

"I'm sure we have time for two simple words," her mother said. "I'm not accustomed to having questions thrown at me in the morning, or any time, without an initial greeting of some kind, no matter who is doing the questioning."

Jana did not reply.

"Oh, for goodness sake. I'm getting as far off the track as you seem to be. We both had better settle down and deal with this thing rationally."

"Mother, I..."

"I'll walk down to the mailbox to check if there is a letter. I'll call back immediately."

Jana sat by the phone, her eyes on her watch. It

shouldn't take more than four minutes, she reasoned: two minutes down and two minutes back.
After five minutes, she began to fret, drawing the
attention of the young mail girl.

"I didn't get one either," the girl said, sympa-
thetically. "That's what it is, isn't it? I see it all the
time. Girls race down here between classes. All
looking for the same thing. Just a piece of paper
with a few words scribbled on it. Half the time they
don't say anything, because the people writing them
don't know how to say what they want to say."

It was seven minutes before the telephone
rang.

"Mother?" Jana was unable to maintain her
composure. "Mother?"

"It's all right, my girl. I have the letter in my
hand. I believe I'm as excited as you seem to be."

"Open it please, Mother."

"It's addressed to both of us, Jana. I'll just scan
it for the message: Things are going to be fine, Glen
says, that is if you don't mind getting married the
minute the new year arrives. He has five days' leave
at New Year's, plus two compassionate days, which
he says he hopes will turn into 'passionate days.'
Glen is becoming quite bold. He would never have
dreamed of disclosing those intimate thoughts when

he was here. Oh, there I go again, interfering in someone's private thoughts...in someone's life. I guess I'm apprenticing for the mother-in-law role already."

"What else, Mother? What else did he say?"

"He loves you...and me too, with some qualifications."

"Oh, Mother, you know what he means. He's joking. I'm glad he's loosening up a little."

"I meant to tell you I was delayed a little because Enoch was sitting on the bench in the cold, by the lilac tree. I brought him with me to the house for a hot cup of tea. For goodness sake! I forgot all about him. He's been sitting in his chair by the oven waiting for his tea.

"'I've won the first skirmish,' Glen says. Here's a separate page telling about the problem related to the first telegram. I'll try to condense it as follows: The Protestant chaplain was sick with a stomach upset a lot of them had - something in the food. Glen missed a compulsory church parade. He had to go before a priest to ask for compassionate leave because the other chaplain was still sick. The priest refused to recommend compassionate leave. Glen reported this to his flying officer, who had already booked time off for him. The instructor took the matter to Group Captain Fullerton. He asked about Glen's performance, then ordered the adjutant to allow him compassionate leave."

"I don't believe we should have that priest perform the ceremony," Jana joked. Her mother chuckled at the other end of the line. "I'll be home in a week."

"There'll need to be some discipline around here if we are to cope with the new arrangements fate has tossed into our path," Mrs. Hillman stated. "But first, there's Enoch."

"Enoch?" she called. The warmth had tricked him into a half sleep. He roused himself and lifted his eyes to her. Those grey eyes were as kind as ever. They had lost the "flash of fire in the wigwam" several years earlier, although Mrs. Hillman observed something akin to it when they had the musical evenings.

"We're going to have a wedding, Enoch," she told him. "Jana and I would like you to give the banquet address if you will."

"In Delaware language?"

It might be the first of its kind, Mrs. Hillman thought. It would be a surprise for some of the twenty or so guests.

"Delaware language...Delaware.... What an interesting proposal. That would provide a unique touch to the celebration. Why not? Why not give the wedding an historic aspect? After all, Jana's great-great-grandfather was among the first Delawares to be brought into the territory by the Moravians. Delaware it will be!"

Enoch's eyes brightened, and a satisfied smile moved across his face. He spoke a few words in Delaware.

"It will be difficult to find all the right words in Delaware," he stated. "There are no ready words to represent some parts in a modern ceremony."

Enoch would find a way. She had always been able to count on him. She would count on him this time, and she would let him do it his way.

XX

The silver of the winter moon lay soft upon the new-fallen snow. Its glow, through the west window, met the warm light of the hanging lamp, to cast a thin halo around Enoch's head as he stood at the banquet table.

His usually placid face held a trace of the joy it

sometimes wore when he felt the goodness of life overflow in his heart.

He caught the attention of most of the assembled guests, as he had planned, by speaking his first words in the Delaware language. Some registered surprise, some curiosity, and some disappointment.

"The words I spoke in the Delaware language are words of greeting. The Delaware language has almost disappeared. But the echoes of the voices remain in my heart, and they are still living voices."

Several of the guests looked confused as they grappled with the strange introduction to Enoch's address. Was a wedding celebration the right place for such words?

Most of the guests knew that Delaware blood coursed through Jana's veins in combination with her white blood. Perhaps Enoch, in his own way, was paying homage to her ancestry.

Enoch surveyed the audience, then continued in the Delaware language. There were few occasions when his voice showed perceptible emotion. Still, one could not but perceive the profound nature of his remarks, even if they were in Delaware.

For several minutes the guests sat respectfully listening to the words Enoch had prepared. Then, as he appeared to be nearing the end of his speech, there was low muttering from one corner of the room.

Mrs. Hillman paid no attention to the muttering, and kept her eyes on the banquet table.

When Enoch was finished, he stood perfectly still for a moment, his eyes scanning the audience. He knew non-Indian people found difficulty in interpreting the philosophy inherent in Indian culture. Perhaps he could help them to understand in English words.

"I will translate, as nearly as I can, the words I spoke in Delaware," he stated. Smiles returned to the faces of most of the guests.

"We are brought together on this winter evening because our nation is at war. My address tries to reflect that fact. It attempts to say something about the nature of human children, which brings wars, and takes our young men away.

"Our species has not yet learned to settle differences by the use of reason.

"Our ancestors had a fierce hunting instinct. I believe, in our evolution, we have retained some of that instinct. I have thought war to be a modern application of the hunting instinct. It is a time when men hunt down and destroy other men." He paused and looked out at the audience.

Most of the guests had a relative of some kind in the military services.

"Our species, and all other things on earth are children of creation. And all things find ways to recognize the benevolence of the creator: the trees murmur in the rustling of their leaves; the birds' voices give thanks; human children gather to celebrate ceremonial rites.

"But human children are like partly trained animals, with lurking potencies for evil.

"The rites Delawares practise to escape the evils which ravage the human spirit may seem stupid and superstitious to the English mind, but they are poetic in their undertones of reasoning." He gave the guests time to ponder what he said, then turned to Jana and Glen.

"When I spoke of mechanisms of escape, I should have explained that they are not designed for physical escape!" His attempt at a small joke brought a chuckle from those who caught the humour of his words.

"It is still the fate of human children to endure the crashing thunder and blinding lightning their lives encounter."

He stopped and looked down at Jana and Glen.

Jana whispered, "He always did like

Beethoven's Sixth." Glen's face registered confusion, then a smile, as he recognized the significance of her remark.

The northern lights, which had been darting through the moonlit sky, now struck at the western horizon in shards of scarlet, green and yellow, exploding in a great curtain which swept over the snowy world and flashed through the window behind Enoch, lending a magic affirmation to the validity of his words.

"What timing!" Jana burst out, her expression audible to all. She slipped an embarrassed smile to Glen when she realized everyone heard her. But her comment did not disturb Enoch, and he continued.

"Calm is restored to our lives. We look again to the time when all things come together, and life will be at its very best." He paused, and seemed to be pondering his next words. "Then, one day we realize that that time has already gone by us, and we didn't notice it. And hearts which sang the words the lips spoke, no longer sing those words."

Mrs. Hillman dropped her head for a moment, then quickly recovered. She scanned the audience and returned her eyes to Enoch. He seemed overcome with emotion, and did not continue immediately.

"Glen is going away," he said. "His heart will take the words from Jana's lips. And Jana's heart will hold the words Glen leaves with her, until both their hearts may sing again the words their lips now whisper."

The guests were noticeably surprised at Enoch's reference to the emotional relationship between Jana and Glen. He paused, seeming astonished that he had made the remarks. Still, it was obvious that he was enjoying the realization of the moment.

"Now we honour two human children whose hearts are young with song and whose lips are warm with words of love." He waited for a moment. "Perhaps some day, all human children will walk in daylight." He did not explain the remark. "I have one more thing to say. I refer to the words I spoke in Delaware the morning Mrs. Hillman introduced me to Glen. The words were: 'I think we will discover each other's thoughts, and we will be pleased.'" He switched his gaze to Glen. "We have discovered much about each other, and I have been pleased."

Glen flung out his arm in enthusiastic recognition of Enoch's remark. His beaming face left no doubt of the feeling in his heart for his friend.

"I thank you," Enoch said. "That is all for now."

Mrs. Hillman rose, as the guests were still trying

to determine the propriety of applause.

"Thank you, Enoch." She stood looking at him for a few seconds saying nothing. The guests were quiet. Then, a few smiles passed between them; then some light talk; and then laughter, as some of Glen's friends joked about his past affairs with girls.

Glen's mother, who had been seated in a shaded area of the room, rose and approached the table, which held a tray of glasses.

"Laura Hansen, you have the rightful honour of calling the first toast to the bride and groom," Mrs. Hillman stated, reaching out to her.

Mrs. Hansen stepped forward, her concern over Glen plainly registered under her reserved smile. She laid one hand on Jana's shoulder and the other on Glen's.

"You are the human children Enoch spoke about. Now you are both my children." She let her hands move down to take their hands, then lifted a glass of wine from the tray. She curled her fingers around the glass, clearly exposing the bruised knuckles the washboard had left her.

"A toast to the children!" she called. When she saw some of the guests staring at her hands, instead of focusing on Jana and Glen, she quickly moved to the outer edge of the circle of light.

Mrs. Hillman gathered a tray of food, and invited

Mrs. Hansen to the privacy of the small den off the living room, where they talked quietly as the guests feasted on corn soup, roast beef and apple pie.

Then...it was over.

Mrs. Hillman watched from the window, as the mailman put Mrs. Hansen in the back of his car with his wife. Ted climbed into the front seat, and the car started toward the road, and the journey home, in the starry brilliance of the winter night.

She looked around the living room once more, then made her way down the hall past the closed door of Jana's room to her own room.

The statistics on battle losses given to the newspapers seldom told the true story, and letters arriving in Canada were so thoroughly censored that people learned very little about the real losses in men and planes.

One statistic which got through to the newspapers told of the Royal Air Force losing more than one hundred planes and five hundred men on one night raid. Some said the statistic was designed to shock the allied countries into greater effort to defeat a vicious enemy, whose strength and determination had been underestimated.

When Glen returned to the air base, four days after the wedding, he discovered that he would get no more leave. The severe losses in Europe made it mandatory that those graduating in February and March would go directly overseas. They would be thrown into battle as soon as their operational training was completed.

The news of the punishing losses and cancelled leaves brought pain to the hearts of many Canadians. Among them: Jana, Laura Hansen, and Katherine Hillman.

XXI

Jana was preoccupied as she rode alongside her mother from the railway station for the Easter holidays. It had been a trying three months. The increased effort demanded to win the war had somehow found its way into the Teachers College. Professors asked far more from the students, even though the increased demands seemed to have little to do with the immediate needs of the war effort.

"What is it, dear?" her mother asked.

"I guess I'm just worried about Glen," Jana replied. "It's devastating when one is worked to death at the college and worried to death at the same time."

"We are all worried, my girl," Mrs. Hillman remarked. "It touches all of us, you know."

Of course her mother was worried. It had been selfish of Jana to think only of herself. And as for Mrs. Hansen, Jana had not even written a note to her in the three months since the wedding. For a moment she wanted to sink down into the seat.

Her mother tapped her on the knee. "It's all right, my girl. We'll get things going when we get home. There are still some good things there to provide some balance."

Home! What a comfortable sound the word had at this moment. *All the comforts of home.* That phrase people used a thousand times without probing the depth of meaning it contained. She had thought of it almost carelessly herself.

She studied her mother for a moment.

"What is it?" her mother questioned. "My hair?"

"Mother, I wasn't paying any attention to your hair."

"It's greying."

"There's not a single strand of grey!"

"No, but it's losing its good red. When that begins we call it greying. Perhaps by the time the colour is gone, what's underneath will be enriched in compensation."

"I wonder if there is compensation for the loss of skin on Mrs. Hansen's knuckles on washday," Jana said.

When Mrs. Hansen proposed the toast at her wedding, Jana had thought of taking Mrs. Hansen's hands in hers. Now she wondered why she had not done this. It could have provided some comfort to Mrs. Hansen when she was being made painfully aware of the stares of some guests.

"We are going to visit her while you're home," her mother stated. "Do you realize we have been to that place only twice? Once when we drove in for the apples and discovered Glen; once in the fall previous to your marriage. We must bring her closer to our family."

"She's very independent. Glen told me that."

"It seems to be a dominant characteristic," Mrs. Hillman remarked. "A rather admirable feature. I believe it gets us through when there's nothing to come to our rescue."

The car turned into the lane past the bench by the lilac and moved slowly toward the house. Jana's eyes scanned the house and the yard, then swung over to the woodlot, resting there for several seconds.

The bare trees held a suggestion of impatience for spring. By the end of the holidays some of their buds would be bursting, and when she came home in the summer their leaves would shade the secret bower.

She wondered if the good things her mother talked about would supply sufficient balance to preserve some meaning to life...to her life which had become so complicated.

As they stood in the yard Tooty Lefevre drove in with the official marriage certificate.

"I thought you'd be home for the holidays," she said. "I needed a chance to get out in the fresh air, a chance to burn the document dust out of my lungs."

Tooty liked to drive in the country to get away from things. And to get away from herself, they suspected. They knew she liked talking to Mrs. Hillman. Mrs. Hillman had often helped her to "straighten her perspecive a little," Tooty said.

Tooty wasn't too worried about the complications of the law. Common sense was the only reasonable law, she said. And where her common sense showed her the direction, she followed it. And the people generally agreed with her. They needed her. Who else would process documents for so little?

There had not been time to fully process the documents before the wedding because Tooty was away. She rushed back in time for the ceremony. When she pronounced the articles ("by the authority vested in me as justice of the peace") there was a quality in the words, a quality absent in the church ceremonies with all the hoopla. Tooty meant every word she said. She felt the words, some said.

Tooty had been devastated by the loss of her husband in the first world war. She drank too much and it robbed her of her good looks. But neither booze nor tragedy had robbed her of the integrity she was known for.

She didn't get many weddings, and with the war, people who might have asked her to marry them, went to the church instead. It would be seen as honouring God, without whom the war might be lost.

It was a warm, quiet morning when Mrs. Hillman and Jana stepped into the car to drive to Mrs. Hansen's place. Jana pulled the car around the bend to the bridge. Down below, three Indian boys stood around a bonfire. Their eyes were fixed on a man leaning heavily over the end of a long pole. The pole, mounted on a tripod of sturdy maple limbs serving as a fulcrum, extended out over the water to a square dip net with wings on two sides. As the sagging bottom of the net broke the surface of the water, two trapped pickerel flashed in the morning sun.

"Fresh pickerel!" Jana exclaimed, excitedly.

"Let's see if we can buy some for Mrs. Hansen," her mother suggested.

On the far side of the bridge a canoe tugged playfully at a rope tethering it to a willow at the water's edge.

Jana thought of the day she and Glen went fishing in the canoe.

"Jana! Aren't you going to stop?"

"I believe I started dreaming a little." Jana applied the brakes forcefully.

"Pauline Johnson again?"

"A little like that, perhaps."

Her mother laid her hand lightly on Jana's arm as she reached for the door.

"Good morning," Mrs. Hillman called, as Ted stepped from the kitchen door with two steaming pails of water.

"Good morning," he replied. "Mama is around at the back washing. I'll tell her you're here. You can come around if you like."

Mrs. Hansen was leaning over the washboard, her grey-streaked hair limp above the steaming tub.

"I must look a sight," she said. "I'm taking advantage of the unusually warm weather to dry the clothes. I'm just about finished. Please sit down on the bench."

She saw the two women glancing at the skirt she wore. "You noticed my skirt, did you? This is something I wrapped around me one day when I had nothing else to put on to do the washing. It was a sugar sack I neglected to bleach in the sun. It still carried bold, red letters saying, 'Let Redpath Sweeten It.' I worried about what my husband might say. He just laughed and squeezed me. After that it became a ritual. I left it on deliberately. It provided a little humour on wash days. And it gave my husband a reason to pat me and say something nice."

Jana helped her to wring out the last of the clothes and hung them on the line. Then it was time for tea.

"Ted, fire up the stove and fill the tea kettle. This tea won't be the high tea of the novels," Mrs. Hansen said, turning to Mrs. Hillman. "But it will be brisk, black tea, with your choice of sugar, milk and cream."

"You do find time to read then, Mrs. Hansen," Mrs. Hillman said.

"I often read the two school library books which circulated each month. It was quiet after the children were in bed."

She stood up straight and dried her hands on her apron. "Please call me Laura," she said.

"And I'm Katherine," Mrs. Hillman responded.

They smiled and studied each other for a moment.

"What a pretty-sounding name Laura Hansen is," Mrs. Hillman remarked.

"I don't think it slips more smoothly from the tongue than does Katherine Hillman," Mrs. Hansen countered. They both laughed.

They sat on the bench under the apple tree, cups in hand, and talked freely in the warmth of the morning.

"Do you enjoy poetry?" Jana asked, reaching for her bag. "I have brought a book of Pauline Johnson's poems. It is called: *The Song My Paddle Sings.* I would be pleased to have you accept it."

The roll of distant thunder grabbed their attention and precluded an immediate reply to Jana's offer.

In the quiet that followed Mrs. Hansen explained that, in her opinion, all good language had the sound of music in it. She was sure that's the way it was with many people, especially those who were trained to hear it. It was reflected in their speech.

"I have tried to learn from such people," she said. "Especially from one fine lady who takes me in her car to our Women's Institute meetings.

"I have made the words of some such people my words also. When I'm doing the washing I sometimes practise imaginary conversations in which I employ the quality words I have learned.

"Those words come in handy with people such as the bank manager. I've watched Mr. Donald change quickly from his gruff demeanour when I employ the best words at my command. He almost smiled once or twice when I negotiated a small loan to get me through until the apples were ready, or until the young roosters were fattened. I guess you might say at such times good words are 'music and money!'"

A crack of thunder, much closer now, and the darkening sky seemed to indicate that a major storm was on the way.

"Your washing! Mrs. Hansen...Laura," Mrs. Hillman reminded her. "May I help you remove it from the line?"

"It will simply get a good rinsing. It will be fine," Mrs. Hansen replied.

The collie scampered under the wide bench and lay whimpering.

"She's frightened of storms, now that she is getting old," Mrs. Hansen remarked. "Ted, take her to the storage shed, then come into the house with us."

"I'm not afraid of a little storm," Ted said.

Mrs. Hansen's determined eyes landed on his.

"All right," he said, turning slowly, flinging his arms out to the sides. "Come on, Bobby. We better hurry."

Ted had barely reached the house when the storm broke with a fury. The rain pounded against the door behind him and lashed the windows in torrents of water.

"It's a strange-looking storm," Mrs. Hansen called, peeking out from behind the curtain. "It looks bad."

Now the sound of heavy rain on the windows was accompanied by the sound of sharp pings. They were scattered at first; then more frequent; then they came in a deafening onslaught as hailstones pounded the roof and the west windows. One of the large windows cracked like a rifle.

Mrs. Hansen grabbed a blanket and suspended it from the curtain rod.

"If the window goes, we won't be showered with glass," she said.

It took only a half-hour to lay a carpet of hailstones four inches deep across the landscape. No one could find words for a few moments, as they stood surveying the scene from the open door.

"The orchard!" Mrs. Hansen cried out. "The young roosters!"

She looked out the back door to the clothesline. Some shredded sheets still clung to the line; other articles were buried in hail. Mrs. Hansen didn't speak for some time. Then she pulled herself up straight.

"Ted, gather up two milk pails full of that hail. We're going to have some homemade ice cream!"

Ted moved awkwardly in his chair before obeying his mother.

Mrs. Hansen fired up the stove, and she was soon stirring a blend of eggs, milk, sugar and vanilla into smooth consistency. She brought the mixture to a near boil, then removed it from the stove to cool, setting it by a bowl of fresh cream she brought from the cupboard.

"Jana, perhaps you would pour some fresh tea for us," Mrs. Hansen suggested.

Jana quickly got up and reached for the tea pot. She was glad her mother-in-law asked her to pour tea.

She arranged the cups and saucers the way she had been taught to do in her early years at the Academy. "A cultured lady is expected to pour tea with sophistication," the instructor stated emphatically. She had felt awkward when it was her turn, and her hand shook so violently the cup rattled in the saucer. That kind of rattling was fine for working men in a mess hall, the middle-aged teacher said, but it was not acceptable when pouring tea for ladies. "Now, get hold of yourself, young lady, and try to develop at least one of the niceties of the social graces!"

Jana smiled when she thought of those early days. The disciplines were now as much a part of her life as brushing her teeth.

"It is not intended to be high tea," she said, half joking, as she saw Mrs. Hansen glance over from the stove a couple of times. "The arrangement is designed to be cosy, and appropriate for the day. Now for the milk, and the ceremony can begin."

Mrs. Hansen looked at the milk pitcher. "I believe we have encountered a problem," she said. "There won't be quite enough milk for my ice cream recipe, not with the cream being as thick as it is."

"Ted," Mrs. Hansen called to the boy stretched out on a couch in the adjoining room. "Ted, get Bobby from the shed and send her to bring the two cows from the woodlot. Then you can strip the Durham. We need extra milk for the ice cream."

Ted was back in a few minutes.

"She won't go," he said. "She doesn't like the cold on her feet."

Mrs. Hansen went to the door. "Bobby! Get back there to the woodlot and bring those cows. Now, get going!"

The dog stood looking at her for a moment, then turned her nose toward the woodlot, sniffed at the cold air, and started off at a slow trot to find the cows. Her feet, still distrusting the unstable footing, slipped sideways occasionally. Soon she gained speed, jumping from side to side in ski fashion, as if having found something new in her world of sameness.

"I think she's enjoying herself," Mrs. Hansen said, turning to the others. She and Bobby had been friends for fourteen years, she reminded herself. The dog needed her support more than ever now. Somehow she felt the need for the friendship of the dog more as the war increased in intensity.

Ted would soon be of conscription age. The government propaganda mill kept spewing out the messages of the need for full effort on the part of the people in winning the war, a war which required increasing sacrifices in young lives.

There were intimidating messages about loyalty. Loyalty to the mother country. Wasn't that the same thing the politicians shouted twenty years earlier when her father was taken? Was there no loyalty due the women whose husbands and sons were taken from them? She looked over at Jana. Was this beautiful girl to be one of those left to live a life of loneliness? Suddenly she realized that her thoughts had strayed far from the dog and the milk she needed.

Ted returned to the house with milk for the ice cream. There would be plenty extra for tea...and for biscuits. She'd make fresh biscuits and top them with ice cream and strawberry jam.

Mrs. Hillman set the small metal pail containing the ice cream ingredients in the larger pail, and packed the space between the pails with hail and a bit of rock salt. "My goodness," she exclaimed suddenly. "We forgot the pickerel!"

"Pickerel?" Mrs. Hansen questioned.

"From the river, this morning. We have two for you also."

"I'll clean the pickerel," Ted said. "I'll clean them all and put Mrs. Hillman's on ice."

"Everyone will be employed in today's projects," Jana stated. "It will be a total effort, as our government spokesmen delight in proclaiming." She began to turn the handle to obtain uniform cooling of the ingredients, and finally the freezing into ice cream.

The meal of fresh pickerel fried in butter, homemade biscuits, and ice cream lingered pleasantly in their thoughts as Mrs. Hillman and Jana drove toward home.

About a mile from the bridge they overtook Jimmy's father walking home from work at the stables. They stopped and offered the bent man a ride.

Mr. Sundol seemed very tired and did not speak until Mrs. Hillman asked him if there was any news of Jimmy from overseas.

"He's all right," Mr. Sundol said simply. "Maybe he'll come home when the killing is finished. Maybe he will not."

Mrs. Hillman didn't know what to say. It was plain to see that the war was profoundly affecting the aging man's life, as it was the lives of all of them. It was strange that she had never thought of Mr. Sundol actually suffering. He seemed to always go about his work in the same quiet way, as if the world were normal. She felt slightly ashamed that she had not included him when she thought of the negative implications of war on the daily lives of people. If Jimmy did not come back, Mr. Sundol would be alone. How was she to reply to Mr. Sundol's statement with anything that would make sense? She still had difficulty sometimes, even after all her years on the reserve, in finding words to fit the Indian mind.

"Jimmy is a fine young man," she said, as Jana pulled the car to a stop in front of Mr. Sundol's place. Mr. Sundol nodded his head once without looking up, then started up the lane to his neat cottage on the hill.

"What is it?" Mrs. Hillman asked. Jana looked ready to cry.

"It was something in his voice. When he said 'maybe he will not.' 'Maybe he'll come home.' It sounds so...hopeless."

They drove the rest of the way home with neither of them saying anything.

"Do you think I'm being a silly girl?" Jana asked, when they arrived at their gate.

Her mother tapped her gently on the wrist. "We're home," she said, quietly.

XXII

Jana walked down the lane to get the morning mail.

The air floating across the meadow from the woodlot was delicately spiced with scents of flowering bushes and tulip trees. The clear calls of songbirds echoed from the thorn thickets and fence rows.

All the elements had arrived on time and in the right proportions for a normal spring.

Spring was the ice cream of the seasons, Jana mused. She stopped by the lilac, threw her head back and let her lungs fill with the lilac-scented air. She held onto it for a moment, as if to get all the goodness from it, then let it go.

She lifted herself up on the balls of her feet and did a pirouette, then tours chaines around the lilac tree, her light skirt spinning out to brush the blossoms.

Her legs coaxed her to dance a ballet sequence from *La Belle Helene*. She whistled her accompaniment and danced until she began to tire. She spun herself back around the lilac tree, did two grands jetés en avant, and brought the performance to a close.

She bowed deeply, and burst into a laugh when she thought of the silliness of it all.

"I'm La Belle Helene, at least for this performance," she said out loud, and laughed again. "I'm La Belle Jana. And I have supped the nectar of a bountiful nature. And that nectar has tricked me into being a silly girl for a delicious few moments. And it's all right, for I am alive, and I am an element in this glorious morning and..."

She slipped the official looking brown envelope from the mailbox. It was addressed to her mother, and bore the stamp of The Department of War Production. For a frightening second she saw only War, but as her eyes became more focussed, she saw the word Production. She hurried to the house and handed the letter to her mother, who was standing at the door.

Mrs. Hillman opened the letter and scanned

the contents. It stated that the Mission Convention, which held title to the farm, had, at the request of the Ministry of War Production, surrendered the land for the duration of the war. It was to be used in a special program involving agriculture. And it would be administered by a government-appointed superintendent. The dwelling would be excluded from the agreement.

"I wonder if we'll still be in that dwelling?" Mrs. Hillman asked.

"What is it, Mother?"

"The land has been removed from our control." She stood quietly, trying to accommodate the message spelled out before her. "That relieves us of the worry about planting and labour."

"The house, Mother...what about the house?"

"The status of the house is not altogether clear. It has not been surrendered in the arrangement. It's possible we may be able to keep it."

"Maybe we'll have to move in with Mrs. Hansen," Jana suggested, and laughed.

"By the way, Ted called from town when you were dancing your way around the lilac tree. He said they would pick at least a half an apple crop this year. The back half of the orchard was hardly touched by the hail."

"Mother, let's have a pot of good tea, and some of Mrs. Hansen's beautiful biscuits with strawberry jam."

"The ice cream will be missing this time," her mother remarked.

Four days after the letter arrived, the chief of the reserve came by. He carried an official document from the Missionary Convention outlining the status of the house. It would be left in the possession of the present occupants, subject to certain conditions. The house must be maintained in good condition, and no alterations were to be allowed. An occupation fee would be levied on the house relative to its value.

"I wonder who they think put the value into this dwelling," Mrs. Hillman fumed. "Still, even with excessive rent, it's better than getting kicked out on the road," she sighed.

"Our band had no alternative but to go along with the authorities," the chief of The Delaware Indian Band stated. "The threat, you know. There's always the intimidation when another group has more power than you have. And the war gives them the excuse to do anything they want to do, and to do it secretly."

"Secretly?"

"There's something not quite right about the takeover of the mission land - your farm. There's something they're not telling us. They don't have to, you see. They've got the power, and it's wartime."

"I think you may be right, Chief Peters. I've been wondering about the vaguely worded statements in the original letter."

"If we're square with people, we expect they'll be square with us," the chief remarked. "It's not always the way it turns out."

"Yes, that's true, unfortunately."

"Mr. Hillman was a good man, and square," the chief stated.

"Yes." Mrs. Hillman's face became placid, then lit in a soft glow. For a few seconds she was back with her husband in the early days. She and Roy were preparing for Jana's entry into the world, and in this very house they had struggled to get ready for her.

"He was a good man, and square," she said.

Mrs. Hillman did not speak for some time, and when she tried to speak, she seemed confused as to what they had been talking about. Then she was silent.

The chief waited.

After a few minutes Mrs. Hillman seemed to find her way back, her speech now only slightly incoherent.

"Are you all right, Mrs. Hillman?"

"I'm sorry. I seem to have lost my train of thought for a moment. I'm fine now.... Roy built this holding into a proud, productive land when it was deserted and returning to wilderness!"

"It might be good not to say anything," the chief suggested. "I thought it would be all right to speak to you. It might help some way."

"Thank you, Chief Peters," Mrs. Hillman called, as he started to walk away, his eyes now more on the ground than on the horizon.

When Glen went into the air force, Enoch tried to find someone to replace him. But most men who were not in the military services were employed in war production of some kind, and good labour was hard to find. Finally, after discussing the situation with Mrs. Hillman, Enoch decided to take a chance on Leland Daniels.

Enoch had known Leland Daniels from the time he and his parents moved into the dilapidated house across the river at the beginning of the Depression.

His parents decided early that Leland would never learn anything in school because he wasn't smart enough, so they had kept him at home. He had never had a job away from home in all his thirty-eight years.

Enoch supervised Leland Daniels closely at first. Then, as the man started to show some competence, Enoch gave him more responsibility. Finally, Enoch left him to do simple jobs on his own. Mr. Daniels had become a "happy worker," Enoch said.

Mrs. Hillman had been putting off telling Mr. Daniels about the loss of the land. Now she could wait no longer. She wondered if he'd understand her when she gave him the message.

At first, Mrs. Hillman thought Enoch should be with her when she gave Mr. Daniels his dismissal notice. She decided against it. She must execute this task herself. She would have to make many decisions on her own.

She walked slowly toward the open doors of the machinery shed where Mr. Daniels was oiling the wheels of the machinery soon to be put to work in the fields.

"Mr. Daniels," she began, "I'm afraid your services will not be required after today." The man looked up, his simple expression indicating he did not understand her statement.

"What?" he said.

"I mean," she said, stumbling over her words, "I mean that you will not have a job here tomorrow."

"Fired," he said.

"No, not fired exactly, "You see..." The slight smile returned to the man's face.

"Good," he said, nodding his head. He picked up the oil can and continued to lubricate the wheels of the seed drill.

"Oh, Mr. Daniels, you don't understand. Do not come to work tomorrow."

A vague bewilderment replaced the man's smile.

"Fired," he said. He put down the oil can, his jaws beginning to imitate a chewing motion. He walked through the wide doors and turned onto the path to the bridge.

"Come back! You can stay until this evening."

"Fired!" He threw his right arm into the air in a half-wave of acknowledgement, slapping at the air with the back of his hand.

"Your pay," Mrs. Hillman reminded him, but he did not respond. She turned back to the drill he was working on. My God, what have I done to that poor man? she thought.

"Damn them!" she shouted. "Damn them for this disruption in peoples' lives! Damn them for compelling me to inflict this cruelty on that unfortunate man; taking from him the only real job he ever had!" She should have asked Enoch to help. The man would have understood Enoch.

Jana was busily thumbing through the pages of the telephone book when Mrs. Hillman reached the house.

"There it is!" Jana exclaimed, "The Department of Education for the Province of Ontario. They're going to hear a new voice when they pick up their telephone in the morning. Today I'll prepare for what I'm going to say. I believe I'm about to enter the world of work."

"We are both thinking along the same lines, apparently."

"It will be the first time in my life I will have earned real income," Jana announced.

"I commend you for your decision, but I remind you that you haven't got a job yet. And there is your year to finish."

"I'll be through in a couple of months with a degree from one of the best schools in the country.

That should make me a whiz at getting a good job."

"The world is still quite wonderful to you, my girl," Mrs. Hillman remarked. "Perhaps you have the right attitude. But we are facing a hard reality now, and that reality is that suddenly we have no income of any sort."

They decided to discuss it over a pot of well-brewed tea.

The last two of Mrs. Hansen's biscuits had been carefully stored. "Hot biscuits with a good cup of tea have diminished many a problem for me," Mrs. Hansen had said.

Mrs. Hillman put the biscuits into the warm oven to freshen them, then went to the cupboard for the butter and strawberry preserves. "Someone must have hidden the strawberry jam," she said.

"Mother, you already placed it on the table."

Jana looked closely at her mother. Those momentary periods of forgetfulness her mother was experiencing were beginning to worry her.

"I read a story once in which one man, describing another man, said, 'He was the ragged end of everything.'"

"Mother!"

"For a fraction of a second I felt myself going in

that direction. It was frightening."

"Mother, we'll be fine. Remember what Mrs. Hansen said."

"Yes, we'll be all right. It was just a momentary lapse when I was off guard," she said, spreading butter over the hot biscuits.

The next morning Jana was on the telephone to Toronto when the roar of a huge truck carrying a bulldozer drowned out the voice on the other end of the line. Mrs. Hillman slammed the kitchen door shut and went to the window. Following closely was another truck carrying lumber, which pulled up behind the first truck. A man stepped down from the passenger side of the lead truck and walked toward the house.

"Madam," the man said, without bothering to greet her, "by order of The Department of National Defense, I hereby advise you that as of today the Department will assume possession of the so-called mission farm, and all properties adjacent to the land, with the exception of the dwelling. I assume there is only one dwelling?"

"Yes."

"There will soon be other dwellings...barracks if you like. They will house the hundreds of Japanese gathered from the settlements in British Columbia. The internees will be required to produce food for the war effort. They will be guarded constantly, so you will have no worry about security."

"There are no captured Japanese soldiers then?"

"No," the man replied, in a bitter tone. "If they were captured soldiers you'd know what they were up to. With these people you can't tell. They could be spies or saboteurs. You can't trust them, so they have to be confined in areas where they can't do any harm. Who knows how much harm they have already done to help the Japanese? They might have had some part in the slaughter of the Canadians at Hong Kong." The man handed her a sheet with printed instructions.

There would be no fraternization and no venturing within five hundred yards of the living quarters. If any suspicious activities were detected while the internees were in the fields, such as attempts to make their way to the river, those activities must be reported immediately to the authorities.

Mrs. Hillman ran her eyes over the list again. Her plan of behaviour was set out for her, and all this before a sod had been turned to build the compound. She had been relegated to a position of spying, with no choice but to comply.

The penetrating glare, absent for a few minutes, returned to the man's fierce blue eyes. He asked her if she had any questions. What he was really saying was: You had better not interfere in any way with the project.

"We will get started on the construction immediately," he said. "Did I inform you that all regulations take effect as of this moment?" He turned toward the trucks which had now been joined by three more trucks loaded with equipment and materials.

"I believe there is an elderly native who has substantial knowledge of this holding. We will require his assistance in determining the drainage patterns and the fertility of the soils. May I leave that message with you?"

He continued toward the trucks, the sound of his heavy boots striking the gravel, emphasizing the message that Enoch was to be conscripted for the project, and she was to be his recruiting officer.

The chief's simple words came back to her: "There's always the threat...when they have more power than you."

Jana burst through the kitchen door and into the yard where her mother was standing.

"I've got a job!" she called. She leapt forward and threw her arms around her mother, spinning her around with her.

"Apparently I'll have a position also, but I doubt that it will be as satisfying as yours," her mother said. She explained the reason for the trucks, and the noise coming from behind the machinery shed.

"My girl, I am exceedingly pleased at this moment to hear what you said, and what I so carelessly dismissed. Please tell me again."

"I have a job, mother, a teaching job. I'll be able to start in September. I'm going to teach the children ballet after school and on Saturdays. I might even start my own ballet school. Wouldn't that be exciting? Let's see, what will I teach first...?"

"Jana, are you forgetting that you have still to graduate?"

"In a few weeks I'll be through. I'll have my degree and I'll be ready to step out into the world of work...and the world of the Arts, if I have my way. Glen will be proud of me." She frowned. "We haven't heard from him in some time. I wonder if..."

"There'll be a letter soon. You know the delays the overseas mails are subject to in these times."

"Well, my neglect in writing him will suffer no

further delays," Jana stated. She plunked her cup down on the table and went directly to the writing desk.

She'd have something new to tell him in this letter. His last letter was thoughtful and generous, even with the cut-out portions. She wondered what those cut-out portions said. She'd have to wait to discover that secret.

There had been no secrets between them the last time he was home. They had specific plans for the three weeks he was entitled to but never got.

She felt a sudden wave of emotion spreading through her. Her heart started to pound wildly against her ribs and her legs fell limp. A cry came from her throat and her body shook.

"Oh, God," she cried.

Is that the way it would be from now on? she asked herself. Until Glen came home?

She let the tip of her tongue seal the letter.

"There," she said, looking at the photograph of Glen in his uniform. "That's the closest thing you'll get to a kiss until you come home." She smiled until she thought of the reality of his situation. "I hope I'm right," she said. She turned the photograph slightly to the side.

She held the letter up to the light to see if the words showed through the thin paper. Then she thought of the futility of such practice. How many eyes would scan her intimate words before those words would be Glen's and his alone?

She put the letter on the table and sat down at the piano. Music not only soothes the savage beast, she thought. It sometimes soothes breasts, savage only in their intense desire to fulfil nature's plan. She took several deep breaths to steady herself.

XXIII

The newspapers carried the headline: CANADIAN HERO SAVES PLANE.

The daily press occasionally carried stories of heroic acts in their coverage of the war. They generally involved an individual in the army, air force, or navy, and seldom concerned the merchant marine, even though the merchant marine was losing far more men than the navy was losing.

The newspapers fed on such stories. They provided hope for a weary public, and told of the quality of the Canadian men and women sent to do battle.

The stories themselves became part of the propaganda that kept the nation geared to the war effort - a war effort directed toward the protection of the mother country, and the preservation of those principles for which the Empire stood.

On this day, one story stood out from the rest, for it told of a crew of a plane surviving almost impossible odds.

A Halifax pathfinder, on a night mission to mark targets for bombers, was hit by incendiary bombs from a higher-flying pathfinder in its own squadron. A raging fire filled the inside of the plane, but the gallant crew beat out the flames with their parachutes, and the engineer restored control of the elevators. The plane zigzagged its way back to England by alternately gunning the port and starboard engines, for there was no rudder control. After the plane landed, an unexploded incendiary bomb was found on top of one of the gas tanks.

Glen Hansen had brought honour and excitement to the people of his community, and for a short time the horror of war was relegated to second place in people's consciousness.

Many were anxious to be associated with the

heroism of a young man they had sent from their community. They were less anxious to be associated with the casualty lists naming young men they also sent from their community. They shied away from thoughts of the destruction, and loss of lives, with which heroism was associated.

The reporters soon found their way to Mrs. Hansen's place. Did you ever think your son would be a hero, Mrs. Hansen? What education did he have when he joined the air force? Why did he pick the air force over the army and navy? What did he like to eat? Was he married? Where was his young wife? Was it true that he had worked several summers on the Moravian mission farm? That Moravian mission farm that was now a Japanese internment camp?

The questions seemed benign at first, but they soon became pointed and personal. And they became tiresome. Mrs. Hansen would be glad when it came to an end.

The pride she felt at first became tempered with the reality of the danger Glen faced in his operations. The graphic details the newspapers outlined daily began to haunt her. She spent many evenings walking in the orchard, trying to free her mind temporarily of the almost constant worry about the war.

"Ted," she called, as he waited in the yard for the neighbour boy to pick him up, "I don't want you to go into the aircrew. I can't risk the loss of both of you."

"Oh, Mother, you worry too much," he responded. "I'll be all right. I'm just the kind they need for the Spitfires."

She knew his remark was spoken in jest. Still, she couldn't be sure what he'd do once he approached the counter in the recruiting office. "Please try to remember," she said.

She turned back to the house. Katherine Hillman would be there soon. It would be a comfort to have her. She seemed to know how to keep a perspective on things. She'd pick a couple of boxes of fresh strawberries. There might still be some left when Jana came home after graduation.

XXIV

The summer passed quickly. Jana barely had time to complete her preparations for teaching in September.

She was exhausted from the long hours of work learning the curriculum. Now, as she started to walk the mile from the mission farm to the school to meet her thirty-five students, she felt a renewal of energy. With her books cradled in her arms, she urged her shoulders up to meet the sun's goodness, slowly rolling them to distribute the warmth penetrating her light dress.

The children standing at the school door grew quiet as she approached them. Some had smiles on their faces; some looked frightened; and some showed no discernible emotion. Those showing no emotion would be the ones she'd have difficulty with, she thought. No! She would not have difficulty with them. She'd get to the bottom of any problems they might have, and act accordingly. "Don't jump to conclusions," the instructor said. She'd try to remember that.

"Good morning," she called, her voice authoritative, yet friendly.

"Good morning, Mrs. Hansen," two of the older children replied.

"You already know my name, then?"

"We do," the two girls said. "Your husband is a hero, isn't he?"

"Well, I...I tell you what. Rather than discuss heroes and heroines now, let's wait until some day when we're studying history." The girls nodded their heads, seeming satisfied. Jana put the key in the lock and opened the door.

"If you'll line up in two rows on the path, I'll put a record on the gramophone, and you can march into the school. How would that be?" The children gave their boisterous approval.

If music soothed the savage beast, it should also soothe the children until she figured out exactly what she should do next, Jana reasoned. She lowered the heavy head of the gramophone to the record, and the *Colonel Bogey March* sprang from the horn.

"We're soldiers," one of the boys called out. "Yeah, we're soldiers," the other boys chorused. "Left, Right. Left, Right. We're marching around the big Japanese camp!"

The first school term was going well, and Jana was happy with the progress, but she found herself becoming increasingly exhausted by the end of the day. Still, autumn had been kind, and Glen's letters were optimistic. Perhaps everything would work out all right. She, like many others, longed for an end to the war, and for a chance to live a normal life.

She walked toward home, her eyes turned to

the woodlot, where the generosity of Indian summer had set the maples ablaze. A smoky fragrance filled the air with intoxicating mellowness.

For a full two weeks, the wind had disappeared, and left a calm which seemed to hold time suspended. Even the bluejays, whose rasping calls normally filled the thorn thickets, now fell silent, victims of a solitude which lay upon the land.

As Jana approached the door, her mother came around the corner from the garden, carrying a basket of potatoes.

"They're lovely this year," she said. "I believe there'll be plenty for winter. I'll leave them in the ground until I'm sure winter is going to set in." She held up a large potato for Jana to see. "They'll look mighty tempting coming from the hot oven with a winter storm raging outside the window."

Jana dropped her books on the table. It was obvious that her mother was worried about the winter. In her own mind she could see the edge of a storm cutting into the mellowness of autumn.

"Oh, Mother, we shouldn't be worried about winter." But the thought of the driving storm did not leave her, and soon all she could see through the window was snow swirling around and drifting against the door, locking her in. She slumped down in a chair with her elbow on the table.

"I believe you're working too hard, my girl," her mother said.

It was true that she had thrown herself into her job, and she had made things work. Maybe she had let herself get run down. "That's when you start looking for things to worry about," Mrs. Hansen said.

"Right now your blood sugar is low, I would guess," her mother said. "I read about blood sugar in the column that tells you how to keep fit, and be more productive in the war effort."

"If only there was some diversion; something rejuvenating; something happy and exciting; something that could free the spirit and let it fly."

"Would this hot chocolate help get your spirit off the ground?" her mother asked, setting two steaming cups on the table.

As they sat, slowly sipping the hot chocolate in the warmth of the kitchen, Jana started to feel a mild restoration. The winter outside the window was beginning to disappear. In a few minutes it was gone, and in its place, a light haze of evening dew was beginning to hug the edge of the forest, and drift softly into the valley.

"Tomorrow I will plan my mission," Jana announced. Her mother look bewildered.

"The ballet classes," she explained. "It's time to get started. I think they'll let me use the school. I'll announce it to the children Monday. By the end of the week I'll know how many students I'll have." Her mother nodded approvingly.

"It will be something exciting to do in the winter," Jana went on. She was already thinking of what she'd do in her first lesson. She smiled to herself. It was going to be a good winter.

Christmas came and went, and the days began to lengthen. And with the lengthening days came re- newed hope. Perhaps this year the war would come to an end.

There were countless newspaper articles in which military authorities hinted of a massive inva- sion of Europe. There had been probes to check enemy defences. Those probes had proven costly in lives. Now it became more important than ever to throw all available resources into air assaults to soften the enemy up for the invasion.

The allied air forces pounded the major cities of the enemy in massive raids both day and night. Losses were heavy, and casualty lists swelled. People tried to justify the losses in their own minds, as they waited for the invasion which would bring a quick end to the war.

Jana sat at the desk, rereading the most recent letter from Glen. He spoke of what he was doing with pride, and as matter-of-factly as she would have told him about doing her job. Had the war just become another job for men? Had they been indoctrinated so thoroughly, that they could think of the destruction of cities, and killing of people, as just a job? If that was the case, would Glen ever be able to think in normal terms again? Would there be a future in which they could continue their lives where they left off? Some flyers had already been returned to Canada badly wounded. Would Glen be one of those?

Jana had kept herself so busy that she hardly noticed the passing of the days as they lengthened into spring and early summer. As she drove across the bridge on the first day of her holidays, she felt a little more hopeful about the future.

She, like many others, had let herself be tricked into thinking the war would soon be over, for the expectation was that the invasion would quickly put an end to it. Now, as she thought of a world without war, life took on a momentary tranquility.

A pair of cardinals chattering from a tree top shook her from the half-dream she had let herself slip into. She stopped the car and listened to the male's repetitious call.

In the past several months, with her head down in her books, she had largely shut out the part of the world where bird songs accompanied the guns of war. Now that part of the world was making its way back into her consciousness.

It was the world Mrs. Hansen lived in every day. She wondered if she would be far enough into that world to be compatible with her. Perhaps she should wait a few days before going to visit her.

"I'm being terribly silly," she said. "I've got to get hold of myself." She sobered at the sound of her own voice. She pulled herself erect. Her foot came down on the clutch, and she reached for the gear shift. She took another look back at the cardinals, still calling from the top of the large maple.

Laura Hansen was coming out of the orchard when Jana drove into the yard. She stopped some distance away and waved as Jana stepped from the car. She stood for a moment looking at her.

"Good morning!" She came forward with a

basket of apples held close to her body. "They're the first of the Red Astrikans, Jana. It's always exciting to pick the first apples of the season. It's a fulfilment of nature's promise. I've wondered, as I looked at the buds in winter, if nature would follow through." She set the basket down and looked over to the car. "Didn't you bring your mother?"

"I thought it well to let her rest this morning."

"Is she ill?"

"She has been having some momentary spells of confusion. Rest seems to help."

Mrs. Hansen eyed Jana carefully as they walked to the house.

"Tell her I'm sorry, will you? I'll send her some of these beauties."

Jana studied Mrs. Hansen as she put the apples into a bag. Her face carried the peculiar lines of worry that seemed to be the property of women with sons overseas. Etched into those lines was the vague acknowledgement that many of those sons would never return. She wanted to put her arms around the woman, but the time did not seem right.

"We've escaped the hail so far," Mrs. Hansen said, rolling a shiny, red apple around in her hand. "Ted may be able to help with the harvest when he's on leave, if he hasn't already gone by then." She slumped down in a chair by the table. "Sometimes I feel like leaving the apples and running away," she said. "Running away so far worry can't find me." She pulled herself up a little. "It's funny how we always think life is going to get better, and it seldom does."

As much as Jana tried, she could find no appropriate words at that moment.

"Jana," Mrs. Hansen said, "you and I both must face the reality of the world if we're going to be any good to each other. There's no use in pretending everything is going to be all right. All you have to do is look at the percentage of airmen killed to get an idea of their chance of survival. We may be the fortunate ones, but there is the other reality, the same reality that took my father in the first world war." She stood up and walked around the table.

"Come here," she said, reaching out to Jana. She put her arms around the girl and held her close for some time. Then she released her and stood back.

"Now, are you going to be my partner, 'til we see this thing through?"

Jana forced a smile and nodded. "Yes," she replied, as tears trickled down her cheeks.

"I can't seem to find tears any more. Sometimes

I wonder about that," Mrs. Hansen said. She picked a half-dozen red apples from the basket.

"We'll make apple sauce out of these. Fresh apple sauce with cream, and warm, homemade bread with fresh butter."

Jana picked up the bag and walked to the car. She turned back and looked at Mrs. Hansen standing in the doorway. Her arms were folded, and her head was tilted slightly to the right. It was a stance she reserved for times of firm resolve.

Jana turned onto the road and drove at a leisurely speed toward home. She let her fingers slide comfortably over the apples on the seat beside her as their sweet aroma rose to surround her in a soft caress. That familiar aroma seemed to represent a reassurance that the bond she and her mother had established with Mrs. Hansen, and which had now been strengthened, would remain secure. It would be there for all of them as they watched and waited, for a reality only a fickle future would disclose.

She brought the car to a stop at the bridge. She walked out to the centre of the bridge and looked down at the calm water. The river had been part of her reality since that beautiful Sunday when she and Glen had gone for a long canoe ride. She would keep it a part of the new reality - a reality that she and Mrs. Hansen would share - a reality she thought she was now prepared to face.

XXV

Two weeks after Jana left Mrs. Hansen's place, she was back again. In her hand was a telegram saying that Glen was missing.

She hurried from the car to find Mrs. Hansen waiting at the door. This time she didn't hesitate. She rushed forward and took the woman in her arms. They stood holding each other for some time before speaking.

"I can't recall a time when life seemed so hopeless." Mrs. Hansen said. "I know you must feel that way too. There's no use in lying to ourselves. Once we get on even ground with each other, we'll be able to see this through. So let's establish our positions, and then we can plan our course."

What she said seemed to make little sense to Jana. She knew her mother-in-law was struggling to find some direction, and her garbled thoughts became garbled words before they could be clarified. It was a symptom of shock. She would recover, and her common sense would be her guide.

"It's good to know exactly how each of us feels," Jana offered. That was the even ground Mrs. Hansen spoke of, she thought. From there, they could try to look rationally at what the future might hold. They couldn't afford to lose perspective. But isn't that what Mrs. Hansen was saying in her own way? About establishing positions, and planning a course?

"We need each other's strength," Mrs. Hansen said. "Without each other's strength, there is danger that depression will become our teacher."

Of course, Mrs. Hansen was right. She had figured it out.

"Let's not go any farther now than saying we're sorry for each other, and let it go at that," Mrs. Hansen suggested. "I'll catch a ride into town with the mailman next week and get out to see your mother. We can't forget her. Besides, she has a kind of strength neither of us seems to possess."

As Jana drove home, she thought of the strangeness of their conversation – a conversation that didn't once mention Glen. And neither of them had thought of Ted. She'd send him a telegram the minute she got home. How should she word the telegram? Maybe she should send the message to his Commanding Officer and let the casualty officer deliver it. No! There was no casualty involved. Why had she thought of such a thing?

Four weeks passed with no word about Glen. The strain was taking its toll on all of them. For the first time since the children were born, Mrs. Hansen walked into the doctor's office.

"I don't think you need anything, Mrs. Hansen," the doctor told her. "Maybe a small sleeping pill. You're stronger than a lot of women who come in with the same concerns you have." He sat thinking for a moment. "In case there is more serious news about Glen...well, you call me, and I'll have something for you."

On the day the telegram came, Mrs. Hillman scanned it, then handed it back to Jana and sent her off to Mrs. Hansen.

"I'll play Beethoven's *Pastorale* while you're away," she said. "I need to feel the reassurance that comes after the storm. I believe I'll leave the back door open, and listen to it in the garden. It will make up for last year, when it was pouring rain on this date."

Jana had forgotten it was her mother's birthday. There seemed to be little change in her condition in the last year, except that she was more forgetful. She had forgotten the recipe for custard pudding one time, and one time when she was at the mailbox she stood for some time looking around, as if she wasn't sure of the way back to the house. She had quickly recovered in each case, and become perfectly normal again. Maybe it was war worry that was causing the trouble.

Some people seemed to be able to block the war out of their minds, at least for short periods. Maybe that blocking process carried over to other things, Jana thought. Maybe that's what was happening with her mother.

After almost six weeks of waiting for word of Glen, Mrs. Hillman's condition seemed to Jana to be worsening. The momentary spells of disorientation worried her. Just take good care of your mother, the doctor told her. As far as he could see, Jana's mother hadn't changed much in the last year. Those periods of disorientation could be caused by worry.

Jana had just got her mother settled for the night when the telephone rang. The station agent said he had a telegram from the R.C.A.F. Casualty

Officer. He would read it if she wished, before he had a messenger deliver it.

"Please do read it," Jana requested.

"The International Red Cross, quoting German Information, states that Sergeant Glen Hansen lost his life July 14, 1943." There was a pause, then the agent added, "I'm sorry." But Jana did not hear the last two words.

The loud crash of the telephone, and the heavy thump of Jana's body on the tile floor woke Mrs. Hillman from her half-sleep. She rose from her bed and staggered to the kitchen.

"Jana!" she yelled. "Get up and tell me what happened!" She quickly realized the irrationality of her demand. She was now fully awake and she rushed to the girl, slumped between the wall and cupboard, with her head down tight to her chest.

"My God, she's choking!" she cried. She grabbed Jana's feet and pulled her away from the wall. As Jana's head hit the floor, a small amount of vomit came from her mouth. She held her head over to the side and waited until she seemed stable. She kept Jana's head turned to the side with one foot to avoid choking and struggled to reach the telephone.

Jana was still unconscious when the doctor arrived. He looked her over, and put his instruments back in his bag.

"She's coming around now. She'll be all right. Don't expect her to be normal for a while. Shock sometimes affects them for weeks. Keep her warm. We don't want to risk pneumonia."

After they put Jana to bed, the doctor asked, "Isn't she the one who collapsed with the news of her father's death?"

"Yes," Mrs. Hillman replied, "She's a very sensitive girl."

The doctor opened the door, and looked to the east, where the first rays of light were lifting the darkness from the tops of the maples. "I'm sorry," he said, without turning back to her. "I'm saying that a lot these days."

It was a full two weeks before Jana recovered sufficiently to come to the kitchen. She had occasionally shown signs of recovery, only to be driven back by a wave of grief which swelled over her, sending her to her bed and the safe haven nature allowed her.

This morning, as she sat sipping the tea her mother had prepared, she appeared restless.

"Will they give me back my teaching job?" she

asked.

"They've never taken it away, Jana," her mother said. "Do you think you'll be ready to go back to work in September?" Jana forced a weak smile, and nodded her head.

"Well then, I have a surprise for you which I've been saving. I have heard rumours that the board has decided to build a new school. It will contain a room for the Arts and a library."

"The Arts? And a library?"

"Two little girls came along yesterday. They wanted to tell you themselves."

"My ballet students?"

"Yes."

Jana felt a faint stirring in her legs, but weakness soon put an end to her momentary enthusiasm, and the tea cup began to grow too heavy for her hand.

Nothing mattered now that life no longer had purpose. Perhaps she had come to the end of a useful life. Perhaps it would be better if it were to.... The hand holding her cup began to shake uncontrollably, splashing the tea on the table and floor.

"Oh, Mother," she called, and the first tears she had been able to shed poured from her eyes. Her mother hastened to her and slipped her arm around her waist. She held her for some time, with neither of them saying anything.

"For a few terrible moments I wanted to end it all," Jana finally said. Her mother tightened her arm and drew the girl closer.

"Listen, my girl," she said quietly, but firmly. "Every woman who has suffered the tragic loss of the man she loved has gone through what you are starting to experience. Because of the war there are thousands in this country going through the same thing at this moment. Some will end their lives. They find themselves in a winter of despair, from which they cannot extract themselves. For them, reality no longer exists. But for the rest of us reality does exist. It's just that we lose direction temporarily, and can't find it." She looked at Jana to see if she understood what she was saying.

"I'll make a fresh pot of tea," she said. She turned toward the stove, then stopped. "I almost forgot. Laura Hansen sent some apple fritters into town with the mailman, and our mailman brought them out this morning. There was a note asking us to come next week."

On the day Glen was reported missing, she and Mrs. Hansen promised each other they would *face the new reality together.*

Now, as Jana looked at herself in the small table mirror, she questioned whether she'd ever find a reality which would give her life meaning.

When she reached for the hair brush, she was startled to see the thinness of her forearm. If there was ever to be a new reality, rebuilding her body, as well as her spirit, would be part of that reality.

She had been up for an hour, the longest period away from her bed so far. She had exhausted most of her strength, and now she worried that she was starting to hallucinate. She put her hands up to her temples and pressed inward to try to stop the images which were forming in her head. The vision of a woman, which started as a misty outline in the background, came rapidly forward and became a clear image of herself, standing alone.

She saw herself precariously balanced at the edge of a high river bank. Some powerful force was demanding that she make a decision there and then, either to turn and face the large world stretching far back from the river, or to take a single step forward, and let herself descend into the void of darkness in the river depths.

The intensity of the vision made the perspiration drip from her forehead, and her body began to tremble uncontrollably. She swung her arm up to wipe the perspiration on the sleeve of her housecoat, then grasped the edge of the table to steady herself.

Suddenly she had to fight for her breath, like she did sometimes as a child, when she grasped at her mother's apron in a fit of crying, and her mother turned away.

She tried to free herself from her chair, to flee to the refuge of her bed, but the strange force held her, persistent in its demand that she decide which direction she would go.

Tears flooded down her cheeks, and she tried to call out to her mother, but no words would come to her lips. Then, after a few minutes, she felt an easing of the force holding her. Gradually a calm settled over her, and again she was able to focus her thoughts.

She began to think of what the doctor had said to her mother about walking. Perhaps walking was the place to start.

Her mother turned from the stove with two cups of tea, and placed them on the table.

"Mother, I...I had..." She looked up at her mother, and put her hands to her temples.

"I glanced at you a couple of times," her mother said, "but I felt I shouldn't interfere," She placed the back of her hand lightly on Jana's forehead. "I believe your fever is broken," she said.

Maybe my spirit has already begun to rebuild itself, Jana thought. It might have been the "cleansing by fire" the two old Indian women who took care of the school talked about. Sometimes, they said, the fire in a fever burns bad things that make the spirit sick. Jana looked at her thin fore-arm, then put her hands down on the sides of the chair and pushed herself up straight.

"Would you take me for a short walk after our tea?" she asked. Her mother nodded.

"Do you think a small slice of one of Mrs. Hansen's apple fritters, with our tea, would give us the added strength walking demands?" Jana asked.

Her mother smiled, and turned to the cup-board.

XXVI

It took another two-and-a-half years, and the sacrifice of tens of thousands of servicemen and women, to bring the war to an end.

Bringing the war to an end also resulted in the destruction of dozens of cities. In one German cultural city, it was reported that up to one hundred and forty thousand people perished in a single night of fire bombing.

Now the wail of sirens across the nation shouted out "victory," instead of "air raid." And every village and hamlet organized its own victory parade. Strutting politicians spoke from hastily built platforms, and preachers stood in line behind them to thank God for the victory.

At the edges of the boisterous crowds were some who could not join in the joyous celebration, for their sons and daughters would never return. For a few hours they were forgotten, pushed aside in the wild charge of a mob gone mad. Later, when the noise abated, there were those who came to them, ashamed, that in the euphoria which had swallowed them up in the mad march, they had forgotten friends who could not feel the pulse of victory.

On the afternoon of a warm autumn day, Jimmy Sundol, wearing his army uniform, turned into the lane of the mission farm, and walked straight to the kitchen door.

"I know about Glen," he said, before Mrs. Hillman, in her surprise, could say anything.

"Oh, Jimmy, I wondered if you might have suffered a wound of some kind, and been lying in a hospital somewhere when the war ended."

"I didn't tell anybody I was on the way home. I guess I wanted to surprise them."

"You are all right, then? You're not..."

"Not a scratch," Jimmy replied. "I wanted to tell you I was back, and tell you I knew about Glen. I know, coming from me, it won't sound right if I say I'm sorry. But I am, you know. I am." His eyes dropped to the ground. Then he looked up at her. "I wish I could say something better than that."

"Jimmy, I understand your feelings, and I appreciate your coming to see us. I'll tell Jana when she comes home." Jimmy nodded his head, and said he'd go.

He had his clothing allowance, and he'd spend a few dollars fixing up the old wreck behind their house, so he could get around and find a job. He'd come back when he got the car fixed. With that, he walked briskly down the lane toward the road. He stopped, and looked for a few seconds at the lilac tree. It had grown a lot, since the last time he and Glen sat there, talking about what they'd do when the war was over.

Jana walked slowly from the school in the late

afternoon, her legs unsteady at the end of the day. She'd soon be home. She wondered how she had gotten through some of those first days back in the classroom in September, with so many students. The trees in the woodlot were already starting to drop their leaves. Their naked limbs would soon reach toward a sun which had grown pale. There would be no colour to light the skies.

Thoughts of the approaching winter sent a shiver through her body, and a mild feeling of despair began to creep over her. She sought desperately for something to dispel it.

Her eyes searched the woodlot, and beyond to the river. The river! But the river would be locked in ice - ice no paddle could break.

To her, the river had always flowed gently in the warmth of summer, with wild flowers lining its banks, and bird calls echoing around its bends.

She stopped abruptly. Pauline Johnson...'The Song my Paddle Sings.' That was the answer! She would read those poems to the children in the special periods after lunch. And she would be with them, floating down the river in a canoe, with birds overhead, singing odes to summer. There would be lots of stories and poems which would take them into summer. Then, one day the winter would be gone.

The fear that struck through her was quickly disappearing. She walked toward the lane, her legs a little more sure. Perhaps she had succumbed momentarily to low blood sugar, she thought. "Low blood sugar will find problems for you," her mother said. "Hot biscuits have diminished many a problem," Mrs. Hansen said. She'd have a cup of steaming hot chocolate as soon as she got home. The biscuits could wait until supper.

When she reached the lane, she saw an old car pulled up near the house. As she came near the door she could hear Jimmy and her mother discussing the internment camp, which was being disassembled. Jimmy had asked for a job, but had been refused. He said he told them to keep their goddamned job; he'd find another one.

"I didn't mean to swear," he said. "I'm going to try to swear less."

"It's understandable that you might feel frustrated in that situation," her mother said.

"I always did swear some, but it got a lot worse in the army. I don't know how I'd have made it through sometimes, without swearing."

"Were you assigned to the infantry?" Mrs. Hillman asked.

"Until I got picked for the special forces. Think of that...me...an Indian, getting picked for the special forces."

"You must have shown exceptional skill."

"The reason they wanted me is because I could move like a cat and put a rabbit's eye out at three hundred yards." He was quiet for a moment.

"Most of the guys with me got killed," he said. "My own buddy got it right between the eyes from a sniper. I jumped from the jeep and searched for that sniper. Then I spotted him behind some scrub. 'You son-of-a-bitch!' I yelled, and ran right at him, jumping sideways to miss the bullets. I was screaming like a mad man. I think I must have been out of my mind." It was some time before he seemed able to continue.

"I blew the top off his head," he said, dropping his eyes to the floor, his voice little more than a whisper. "His grey brains and red blood were scattered all over. Then I got sick, seeing what I had done. And I wondered how I ever got to the point where I could kill a young man like myself. And then I thought of the goddamned bastards of generals and politicians, on both sides, sending young men to kill each other.

"'You goddamned bastards!' I screamed. 'You

goddamned bastards!' Then I fell down by that German soldier and cried."

"Oh, Jimmy," Jana said, "I..." But she could not go on. She walked over to him and put her hand on his shoulder as he sat slumped at the kitchen table.

"I'll make some hot tea," Mrs. Hillman said.

When Jimmy left, he said he was going up to the northern county to see about a job. They were building some dredge cuts to drain the flat land, he said.

It was almost a year before Jimmy drove in the lane again. He had started back for the dredging company after spending the winter up north in a lumber camp. He had saved quite a lot of money, he said. He was going to trade school in the fall, on his veteran's credits. He was going to amount to something, he said.

As Jimmy sat at the table, Mrs. Hillman could see a change in his face. The wildness that was in his eyes the last visit had been replaced by a more disciplined look. Now those eyes seemed to be looking toward a future and away from the war.

"I've gotten to know the old man better," Jimmy stated. "It'll be hard to leave him all alone when I go to school in the fall. He's getting older."

"Does your father still work at the stables?" Mrs. Hillman enquired.

"Yeah, he still goes down there every day to smell the horseshit."

Mrs. Hillman dropped her head in a little smile.

"It's a wonder places like that didn't close down during the war," Jimmy said.

"Some of the horses were used to patrol the rough areas around the internment camp, I believe," Mrs. Hillman stated.

"It was a method used by a couple of young men from town to avoid conscription," Jana said. "Essential to the war effort, or some such thing."

"Better than riding tanks," Jimmy remarked.

"I understand they're having a big horse show before long," Mrs. Hillman said, changing the subject.

"Yeah, the old man says they're coming from the States and all over. They'll keep him there, working the hell out of him twenty-four hours a day while it's on." He looked out the window in the direction of the stables. "To me, a horse show is just a bunch of horses showing their asses to a bunch of horses' asses showing their horses."

Mrs. Hillman snickered, dropping her head to

the side. Jana giggled a couple of times, then broke into a laugh.

It was a laugh that would not be controlled. She threw her head back, her eyes to the ceiling, her mouth wide open, as gusts of laughter filled the air above her. She stopped to gulp in quick breaths of air, then started again, her diaphragm bouncing until her stomach muscles stiffened with pain. When it was over, she sat exhausted, her deep breathing sobering her flushed face. It was the first time she had laughed joyously since Glen's death.

"Jimmy," she said, "You have no idea what your statement did to me."

But he did have an idea, and he was glad for her. Maybe the war had started to end for all of them, he thought.

Jimmy would never again sit in the comfort of Mrs. Hillman's kitchen. As the war was beginning to end for him, another enemy which he could not see was approaching. Jimmy died in the dark waters of a dredge cut he helped to construct.

Some said Jimmy should not have been working so much overtime and letting himself become so fatigued. On that last night he drove into town for gasoline. He was almost back at the job site when sleep overtook him and he drove off the road into the water-filled dredge cut. In the deep blackness of the cut, he could find no direction and his lungs filled with water.

PART TWO

XXVII

The war had been over for ten years.

Jana had been teaching almost twelve years. She wondered where the time had gone.

She hated having to put her mother in the nursing home. She had waited until there was no longer a reality to her mother's world.

Several times in the two years since her mother's death, she had considered getting a teaching job in London where she would be more in touch with the Arts...and people. "A healthy girl like you shouldn't be living by yourself," the doctor said.

Ted had introduced her to a young engineer working for his company. At one point she thought she might be falling in love with him, and she had stayed with him in the city on two weekends. His heavy drinking put an end to the relationship.

As Jana reached to turn out the kitchen light, the telephone rang.

"It's Ted," came the voice on the line. "I've discovered something I'm sure will please you. I know it's late, but I got so excited I had to call you from our Edmonton office as soon as I got in. I'm here doing some extra work for the seismic crew."

"What in the world are you talking about?" Jana demanded. Ted always did have a way of holding her in suspense until the last minute.

"I'm not joking," he said seriously. "I was going over some geological maps of the Northwest Territories, and I found a Hansen Lake."

"There must be hundreds of Hansens. It's probably named for an old prospector."

"Nope. This lake is ours. I checked with Ottawa. This lake is named for Glen. It's one of those lakes named for decorated servicemen killed in the war."

"What...what do we do now? What does it all mean?"

"It means the lake will carry Glen's name forever," Ted stated proudly.

"Please tell me where it is, so I can picture it in my mind."

"As near as I can figure by the map scale, it's about three hundred and fifty miles north of Yellowknife, not far from Great Bear."

Jana reached for the atlas on the shelf above her desk. She found Great Bear Lake, and marked a spot above it with an X. A mild foreboding came over her, as her pencil marked out the letters spelling Hansen Lake. She drew a couple of deep breaths, and put the phone back to her ear.

"I'm going to phone Bob Conlon in Yellowknife in the morning." Ted said. "I flew with him several times in the High Arctic Islands. He might have flown over the area on his way up there. I'll let you know what he says. Maybe we could arrange a flight to see the lake this summer. I'll let you know..."

Jana pictured a blue lake sitting peacefully in the barren tundra. She could already see the wild flowers springing forth, carpeting its shores in the short summer. That night, as she lay in her bed, she imagined herself drifting over the lake's calm surface in a canoe. The wild birds called out above her. And in the distance some caribou were peacefully grazing.

That vision took her comfortably into sleep.

Jana heard no more from Ted for two weeks. Then, as she was leaving for school, the phone rang. Ted called from Edmonton to tell her he had almost completed arrangements for flying up to the lake. Bob Conlon had recommended the people at the seaplane base. They had good float planes.

"It'll be a Cessna with long-range capability," Ted said. "Are you prepared to go near the end of

July?"

"I'll be ready," she said. There would be nothing to stop her. She'd be on holidays from school.

"I'll get back to you when it gets near the time," Ted told her. "Pack up a few summer clothes, a good pair of boots and a warm jacket. I'll arrange for anything else you might need."

Jana stepped up to the counter at Toronto Airport.

The six weeks of waiting, before Ted called saying everything was ready, had seemed like six months. Now she felt the blood pulsing into her neck, sending a flush to her cheeks.

"Are you all right?" the girl at the counter asked.

"I'm fine, thanks. My name is Jana Hansen."

"Let's see...here we are...Toronto to Edmonton and Yellowknife." She handed the ticket to Jana. "Are you sure you're all right?" she asked again.

"It's just the excitement of it all," Jana replied. "It's my first time on a plane."

"You've got a thrill coming," the girl remarked. "It's a wonderful experience."

"I'm sure it is," Jana said. "And I have another..." She stopped short. The other experience was private. It belonged to her alone. It would not be shared with anybody.

On the way to Edmonton she let her eyes search the land below, trying to imagine what the tundra country around the lake might look like. The book she got from the library told quite a lot about the Arctic explorers, but didn't say much about vegetation. She'd count on the book Ted said he'd have, to learn about the flowers and plants.

She had not been able to see much of the detail of the prairie, she told Ted, who was waiting to join her at the Edmonton Airport. She could identify fields of wheat, and some spotty growths of trees scattered across the plains.

"They're aspens," Ted said. "Like our poplars. They're hanging onto the stream banks where they can get a little moisture. In the north we'll see mostly conifers. They'll be pretty thin in that country on the way to the lake, but I've heard there's enough to spread forest fires in a dry year like this."

When they arrived in Yellowknife, they went directly to the hotel Bob had recommended. Early the next morning they would go down to the seaplane base, and if the weather was good, they'd climb aboard the float plane and fly north to find the lake which carried Glen's name. It would be hard to wait until morning.

Ted had been called down to the seaplane base to confirm the arrangements. Everything was ready, they said. Mark would be their pilot. Be sure to bring a substantial lunch, they told him. There was no telling how long it would be before they got back, especially if the weather closed in.

At seven o'clock the next morning they left for the base. By eight, they were packed into the Cessna with their cameras and their lunch. Jana was in the copilot's seat. She had started to crawl into the back seat, where there was room for one amongst the extra cans of airplane gas.

"No," Ted said. "I want you to ride up front. You have a right to be the first to see the lake."

The pilot was a young, blond-haired man with a Finnish name. He'd be about twenty-four, Ted said, as the young man started the plane's engine to let it warm up. Mark was meticulous in his final check before he pushed the throttle, sending them out onto the lake. The plane, "loaded to the hilt with gas," the mechanic said, rose up on its pontoons, and skimmed the water until it reached flying speed, then lifted into the cool air.

They could see the towering headframe of the gold mine as they gained altitude and swung north toward the lake. It would be at least three hours,

Mark said, before they came to Great Bear. Then they'd have another fifty miles, according to the aeronautical maps, before they reached what he assumed would be Hansen Lake. It was his first trip to that particular part of the territory, he said.

Below them was a forest fire, which had burned for most of the summer, the radio said. It jumped amongst the scattered trees, occasionally exploding one of them into flame.

Soon the smoke from the fires lay behind them, and the land became a careless tartan of brown hills and lakes strung together by streams and rivers. There were waterfalls which hung like silver necklaces from the lips of escarpments, carved and sheared by great sheets of ice, in thousands of years of glaciation.

The ice had left one hundred thousand lakes, the geologists said. Some were so small a canoe could traverse them in a few minutes; some were so large they could hold battle ships.

The immensity of the land staggered Jana. The closeness of the forest and river at home had always made her feel secure. Now, this great space filled her with a sense of unease. Could she ever feel an intimacy with the lake in a land so large - a land they said was cruel, and quickly brought an end to those who neglected its laws? For a few moments she wished that a cloud cover might obscure the lake, and they'd have to turn back.

Mark noticed her apprehension. "It takes a while to get used to this land," he said. "On my first flights, I kept wanting to turn back to Yellowknife. It was frightening when I was all alone." He smiled at her. "It's funny how you get to know the land, and the apprehension disappears. It even begins to feel friendly. But you keep in the back of your mind the reality of the land...the danger.

"This land shows me something new every time I fly over it: the migrating caribou, and the other animals like the grizzlies, the wolves and foxes. In the spring, when the returning sun breaks the grip of winter, the streams and lakes become a string of jewels. The ducks and geese come back. And on the land, life returns with astounding rapidity, in a glorious profusion of plants and flowers."

"Great Bear," Ted called from the back seat.

"That's Port Radium ahead," Mark stated. "We're going around the eastern end. It's pretty wide here according to the map, maybe fifty miles. I'll follow the shore of Dease Arm. It should be clear over the water."

As they rounded the end of the lake and turned

north, they could see a cloud cover not far ahead.

"We'll swing to the west and see if we can find a gap. The clouds don't seem very thick," Mark stated.

After about fifteen miles, they were about to turn back when a small opening appeared on their right. Mark circled around and slipped through the narrow gap. To the north, the sky was clear.

Mark looked at his map and agreed with Ted that the lake showing up a few miles ahead must be the lake they were looking for. It must be Hansen Lake.

"That's it!" Ted called excitedly, as they approached the lake. Jana felt her heart pounding against her ribs. Then she got hold of herself.

In a pocket reservoir, surrounded by gentle hills and tundra, the lake lay calm and serene, its pastel, blue water stretching far to the north.

Mark crisscrossed the lake, looking for a safe place to land. He was watching for obstacles which might be in the landing path, he said. Finally he was satisfied, and he brought the plane close to the surface. He throttled back as the pontoons skimmed the water, sending a silver spray over the windshield.

Jana trembled. It was hopeless to try to compose herself. A long wail rose from her throat, and she fell back against the seat.

After a few minutes, she wiped the tears from her eyes and pulled herself up straight.

"I'm all right now," she said. Ted patted her shoulder lightly, as Mark taxied the Cessna toward a gentle gravel incline at the water's edge. The pontoons scrubbed the pebbly gravel, anchoring the plane as it came to a stop.

Mark climbed down onto a pontoon and stepped ashore. He pushed the plane back, turned it around from a wing tip, and anchored the backs of the pontoons on shore.

Jana was weaker than she thought when she stepped down onto the pontoon. For a few seconds she hesitated, then she slowly lowered her foot, and let her toe gingerly touch the gravel. Gradually she let her foot down flat on the surface. She pressed the ground firmly, as if to test the solidity of the pebbly material.

By the time Ted alighted from the plane, Jana was starting to climb toward a large rock at the top of the bank where some alpine roses had found a sheltered spot to cling to life.

She quickly scanned the lake from end to end, then set out to explore as much of the land along its shores as she could in the time available.

She soon found her steps accelerating uninten-
tionally. She wondered if she might be losing the
mild apprehension she started with. She would try
to remember what Mark said about the reality of the
land.

The tundra spread out before her in a blanket
of muskeg, punctuated by small streams, and pockets of water caught in hollows left by the retreating
ice.

In the distance, three caribou loped along, then
frolicked down an incline and out of sight.

Around her feet lay a carpet of purple flowers
which she identified as saxifrage from her small
reference book. The flowers reminded her a little of
the violets at home. Scattered among the saxifrage
were dwarf willows, their knurled, crooked branches
a measure of their desperate struggle to maintain
their tenuous hold on life.

Holes were tunnelled into the banks where
small animals found safety from the wolves and
bears. Larger burrows likely led to dens where
wolves raised their young, Jana thought.

After some time she came to a small peninsula
jutting out into the lake. For a moment, she debated
whether or not she should walk out to the end of it.

She looked back at the plane, now a yellow

patch at the far end of the lake. She had wandered much farther than she had intended. They would have to leave by three o'clock, Mark said. She checked her watch. It would be after three when she got back. She stepped out quickly onto the spongy muskeg, toward the plane.

Ted had a two-foot lake trout to show her when she returned. Blood trickled from its gills as he held it up for her to see.

"I'll wash it off," Ted said quickly.

Mark was indicating that he was anxious and ready to go. He had checked the plane over and everything was in order. He shuffled around, waiting for Jana and Ted to get their things together. As they were about to climb into the plane, Jana turned back to him.

"May I climb to the top of the bank and take one more look? It's unlikely that I shall ever see Hansen Lake again."

"Sure," Mark said. "I just want some reserve in case we run into a head wind and have to put down on some lake to pour in the extra gas. Fifteen minutes won't make much difference."

Jana scrambled to the top of the bank, where the large rock sheltered the alpine roses. She let her eyes move slowly, reaching across the lake from end to end, registering it indelibly in her mind.

Two ducks splashed down on the far side of the lake, disappearing into the vegetation where their nest was hidden. That nest likely held young duck-lings by this time, Jana reasoned.

From her vantage point, she could see the three caribou in a hollow, their noses testing for some-thing the light east wind was bringing them.

On her way back to the plane, she stumbled across the remnants of a sod house. Its dried pieces of muskeg lay scattered in a profusion of saxifrage below a sheltering cliff.

She swung her eyes over the lake once more. It was just as she had imprinted it in her mind. That's the way she would keep it forever.

As Mark made a wide circle over the land to the northeast, they could see four people walking to-ward the lake. They were accompanied by some dogs, and carried packs, and what looked to be a small kayak.

"They're likely women and kids," Mark said. "My boss says they come to the lakes sometimes to fish when food is short, or when there are some too old to go out on the ice for the summer seal hunt."

Bob Conlon was waiting for them when Mark put the plane down at Yellowknife. He had a message for Ted.

"They want you to fly up to Tuk. Something to do with offshore land they said." He turned to Jana. "If you ever need help in the future, give me a call. I expect I'll be around here from now on. The mining companies are starting to get serious about this country."

On the way to the airport, Jana said she would like to place a bronze plaque on the large rock near the end of Hansen Lake, where they anchored the plane.

"That would have serious implications," Ted said. "It would be difficult, if not impossible, what with government regulations and bureaucratic red tape."

Jana would forget about it for now. Did it really matter? she asked herself.

Ted took her to her plane, and said goodbye. She sat down and put on her seat belt. She looked out at him, standing alone on the baggage cart, smiling and waving energetically, as her plane started to move out to the runway.

She'd be flying back to Edmonton alone. But she wouldn't really be alone. She would be taking the lake with her.

PART THREE

XXVIII

The headlines read: WIDE-SWEEPING NAME CHANGES IN NORTH. Many place names in the Arctic would disappear. Even those places named for early explorers, such as Frobisher, would have their names struck from the maps. Aboriginal names would replace them.

It was an irresponsible act; a blatant violation of tradition; a destruction of history, some said. Others said the changes were justified, and in accord with judgements in land claim settlements. Regardless of criticism, the plan would go ahead, the government officials stated. And overnight, the radio and television stations, along with the newspapers, adopted the new names.

Jana was in mild shock for several minutes after hearing the announcement on the radio. What would it mean for Hansen Lake? she questioned.

It had been fifteen years since she and Ted made the pilgrimage to the lake.

There was something strange, Jana thought, about the announcement of the name changes appearing at the same time as news of increasing mining exploration in the Territories.

Now, after a month with no clear indication of

whether or not there might be a relationship between these two factors, she picked up the phone.

"Ted, I want you to determine what these name
changes and mining exploration activities mean. I'm
starting to worry about the lake."

"The name changes shouldn't affect the lake,"
Ted said. "The exploration is a different matter. I've
been a little concerned about that myself."

"What should we do?" Jana demanded.

"I'll do some quiet investigating," Ted stated. "I
know some geologists working up there. I think I'll
be able to get a pretty good picture of what's going
on."

"Inform me immediately if you detect any
scheme that would adversely affect the lake. I'm
sorry for being so abrupt. It's just that I have a
strange sense that there may be something happening there, and we know nothing about it."

"Jana, we're going to have to approach this
thing with some discipline. Do you understand?
We're dealing with powerful interests - outfits that
are backed by millions.

"It would be difficult prying information out of
any of them involved in planning and policy making. All we'll have to go on is what my geologist
friends are willing to tell me, and that won't be

much, but it may be enough to satisfy us for the time being."

"Ted, I guess I was letting my imagination rush this into a critical situation, on the basis of little or no substantive evidence of wrongdoing."

"I hope you remember what I said." Ted sounded a little upset. "There's something about this you seem to have forgotten. That lake means as much to me as it does to you!"

With that he hung up.

XXIX

News of mining exploration in the Territories had been scarce since Jana and Ted first discussed it a year earlier. Then, on a late afternoon in May, a dramatic announcement interrupted radio and television programs: DIAMOND STRIKE IN NORTH-WEST TERRITORIES. The bulletin travelled around the globe in a matter of minutes.

Eyes knowing little of Canada now scanned atlases for some place called The District of Kee-watin. And soon, speculators were sinking millions of dollars in mining ventures, on the basis of the newspaper stories alone.

Northern politicians got their pictures in the papers, alongside mining men. There was potential for great wealth, they said, and a better life for all the people.

"We need development in the Territories, and we've got to be prepared to make adjustments if that's what it takes," the politicians stated, in response to the few who registered concern for the natural environment, and advised caution.

It seemed that consideration for the land and animals which had given life to the people for thousands of years, would, for the moment, be pushed aside in the fierce race for wealth.

Jana was working at her desk after school, with the radio playing classical music in the background. The music ended abruptly, drawing her attention.

The bulletin announcing the diamond discovery sent a shock wave through her, momentarily riveting her to her chair. What would be the effect on Hansen Lake? After a few minutes she got up and went to the window.

She stood for some time looking out at the quiet, green fields stretching away to the northern horizon. Perhaps she had over-reacted to the announcement.

Ted had kept her informed as best he could. He

had not uncovered anything of an alarming nature where the lake was concerned. As far as he knew, nothing had been discovered on the mining properties a few kilometres from the lake. It was base metals they were after, he thought. And there was some delay because of native land claims.

Jana closed her books and got up from the desk. In another month she'd be leaving that desk for the summer holidays.

It had been a hard year. She'd be glad for a chance to relax, and be rid of all the daily obligations.

She walked out into the early evening and started for home. She found herself pausing frequently and taking deep breaths of the fragrant air. Just around the bend, the full-blossomed lilac would come into view, and then...she'd be home.

She could not remember ever having felt closer to the land and the water, the air, and the sky. When it came down to it, she thought, you could never be closer to anything than the land which gave you birth; which nourished your body and your soul; which was always there - the only thing in existence which had any permanence. Everything else was a dream. How could we ever think of being inconsiderate, or careless of the only thing which gave our lives foundation? she asked herself.

The words on the radio still echoed faintly in her mind as she turned into the lane. She sat down on the bench to rest for a moment in the soft fragrance of the lilac blossoms.

She would try to forget the report, and concentrate on the warmth and security of home, and the cup of hot chocolate she would soon have.

"Jana, I had a call from a geologist friend of mine last night," Ted reported, when he called, two weeks after the announcement of the diamond strike. "This thing is much closer to home than I imagined."

"What's happened?" Jana demanded. "Sorry. Go on."

"The company that owns the leases in the area surrounding the lake intends to do extensive exploration."

"Will they be excavating?"

"That, and draining some of the small lakes, so they can get at the pipes."

"Tell me what you're talking about. What are pipes, and what has that to do with our lake?"

"It's not our lake, Jana. You've got to remember that. It carries Glen's name, and it's ours in that sense only."

But it was her lake in more than name. That lake had been a part of her since the day she discovered it. Now something threatened to tear it away from her. She would never surrender any part of the lake, no matter what forces were pitted against her! She would protect it with her life, if it came to that!

"Jana, are you all right?" Ted asked. "I was about to explain about the pipes."

"I guess the shock staggered me for a minute," Jana replied. "I'll be all right. Please continue. It would be well for me to learn as much as I can, in case there's a confrontation. What about those pipes you spoke of?"

Ted explained that the pipes were areas of softer intrusive rock, which glaciation ground down to a lower level than the harder surrounding rock. Those hollows filled with water and created lakes.

"But our lake is much too large for any draining operation," Jana insisted.

"Horizontal tunnelling would take care of that."

"So we are not in the clear. The lake may be in jeopardy?"

"I regret to say it may be," Ted stated.

"What shall we do?"

"It will take some time to develop a strategy," Ted said. "Disciplined strategy. It may end up in a hell of a court battle, but it's worth a fight if it comes to that."

It was worth a fight all right, Jana said to herself. "Disciplined strategy," Ted said. She would be ready...and disciplined.

She undressed and got into bed, but sleep eluded her. When she rose to get a sedative, she discovered she had forgotten to put on her nightgown. She smiled at the thought of it. Where was the discipline they had talked about?

In the morning she would set a strategy, plan a course. That's when she would require direction...and discipline.

XXX

At seven in the morning Bob Conlon climbed into his helicopter. He had his hand on the throttle, ready to start the engine, when he got a radio call asking him to return to the hangar.

"What is it?" he enquired impatiently. The office girl said there was a call from some woman in the south who demanded to speak to him.

"What's her name?"

"Hansen. I believe that's what she said."

Bob calmed himself.

"I wondered how long it would be before we'd hear from her." He climbed down from the pilot's seat and walked back to the hangar.

"All right, I guess I'd better speak to her." He glanced at his watch.

"Your office phone?"

"I'd better, for this one." He shut the door behind him and picked up the phone. "Bob Conlon here."

"It's Jana Hansen, Bob. When I met you at the seaplane base you offered to be of assistance if ever I should need you."

"I meant what I said," Bob stated.

"I need your help now," Jana said.

"How can I help you?"

"I'm coming up to claim Hansen Lake," she said. "I'll need whatever it requires to camp by the lake for the summer."

Bob hesitated. She might well perish out there all alone. Then he remembered the Inuit family camped on the west side of Hansen Lake.

"You'll have company," he said.

"The kind I don't need," Jana remarked.

"I don't mean exploration crews," Bob explained. "There are some Inuits camped on the west side of the lake. I think it's a family fishing for the summer. If they weren't there, I'd be reluctant to put you by that lake in a tent, even with two loaded rifles. You've got to keep in mind the reality of that country. It doesn't give you a second chance if you make a mistake."

"I'm sure I would be compatible with the Eskimos, and we could look out for each other."

Bob smiled to himself. She was another one of the southerners for whom life is so simple, so ordered. At least she had a degree of justification for her venture into that unforgiving land. He would shout "Beware!" in terms which he thought she would understand.

She was an intelligent woman. And...she was beautiful. He discovered that when she and Ted climbed out of the Cessna, on their return from Hansen Lake. The deep red hue of the evening sun fell upon her face, enhancing a radiant warmth.

"I'll get Bonnie to order all the supplies you'll need," Bob told her. "We'll take care of the other things when you get here."

Mark put the plane down on the smooth, blue

water and taxied to the shore.

The supplies were waiting for them near the big rock, not far from the remains of the sod house, and not far from where the Inuits were camped with two dogs.

Mark made sure the tent was secure and that the supplies were safely stored. He said goodbye, and walked back to the plane. He raised his foot to the pontoon, then turned and looked back. Jana stood by the tent, waiting to see him off.

"Good luck!" He waved, then stepped up onto the pontoon, and climbed into the cockpit. The Cessna roared out across the water and lifted into the air. It circled the camp, then turned south toward Yellowknife.

Jana walked into the sturdy tent and surveyed the equipment. Her eyes stopped at the two rifles slung by the door. They were meant to be used only in an emergency.

She had watched her father clean his deer rifle several times, and he had let her shoot it once during target practice. The loud crack had frightened her.

She took down the rifles and removed the clips, then slipped them back in place, carefully following the instructions Mark had given her. She'd be comfortable with the rifles if she ever needed them for a grizzly, or a polar bear wandering in a hundred miles from the ice.

Now she would need to get prepared for her first night alone on the tundra. She unrolled the Arctic sleeping bag and spread it out on the tent floor. She had never slept in a sleeping bag. She eyed it for a moment, then crawled into it. She soon began to feel its warmth and comfort.

She was glad Bob had arranged for the things she would need. And she was glad the Inuits were camped only a few hundred yards away. Things were working out the way they should, she thought, as she drifted into sleep in the Arctic night.

Jana stepped out of the tent the next morning and looked toward the Inuit camp. Two children, accompanied by two dogs, were halfway to her tent. They stopped a few yards from her. The girl would be about seven and the boy about nine, she thought.

"What are your names?" she asked.

"Sammy," the boy said. "Jeannie," the girl stated.

"My name is Jana."

The children laughed.

"We're going to be neighbours," Jana remarked. Sammy and Jeannie looked confused.

"Friends," Jana explained.

"Friends...ah..." Jeannie reached out her hand and urged Jana in the direction of the caribou skin tent, about two hundred yards down the shore.

Inside the tent, an old Inuit woman with a placid face was busy chewing on a small piece of hide. By her side were moccasins with coloured embroidery on the toes. She looked up briefly and squeezed her eyes a little, then went back to her chewing.

Behind the tent a young woman was cleaning fish. Beside her was a small kayak, propped up on a rock. The woman looked up and smiled when she saw Jana.

"English?"

"Yes," Jana said.

"We will talk," the woman said.

"My name is Jana."

"Christine." She held out a piece of fish for Jana, at the same time putting a small piece in her mouth.

"Oh, I...couldn't eat it raw," Jana said.

"English," the woman remarked. She laughed, and went on cleaning fish.

"The lady in the tent," Jana enquired hesitantly, "Is she your grandmother?"

"Grandmother...mother." Jana was confused. The woman put four marks in the sand. "Children, mother, grandmother, mother."

"Great-grandmother?" The woman nodded her head. She went into the tent and brought the old lady out.

"Her name is Christine," the young woman said. The old lady looked carefully at Jana's eyes.

"Eskimo?" she asked, turning to the younger woman. The young woman looked questioningly at Jana.

"Oh, no," Jana responded, when she realized the old lady saw something besides Anglo-Saxon features, "I...I am part-Indian."

"Good Indian?" the old lady asked, turning to the young woman.

"Yes," the young woman said, smiling, "Good Indian."

What did it all mean? Jana wondered. The answer came quickly, when the old lady went into the tent and returned with a new pair of moccasins.

"Yours," she said.

Jeannie carried the moccasins, as the children walked Jana back to her tent. She gave each of them a stick of gum, and they went home. Tomorrow, Jana thought, I'll have them come to my place for tea.

The next morning the children came again to Jana's tent. Their mother had sent them to bring her to their tent for tea, with her and the old lady.

It didn't take long to find out that the old Inuit woman had a strong attachment to the lake.

"She was born here during the southern migra- tion of the caribou," the young woman said. "She has been here for many seasons of the caribou, in spring and in autumn. She is about 95 years old, we think," she said, looking over at the old woman.

"Many seasons of the caribou," the old woman said, a little smile crowding the wrinkles around her eyes.

"Her...great-grandmother was at this lake when the first white man came back from the northern ocean," the young woman said. "She saved him and his Indian men from starvation."

"Many of the early explorers lacked the humility to adopt native methods of survival, it seems," Jana remarked.

"Now I want to tell you about the canoe," the young woman said, abruptly changing the subject.

"Canoe?" Jana questioned.

"The white men's canoe. White men come from far south most years to fish. They leave their canoe here, and we are allowed to use it."

"But I have seen no canoe," Jana said. Perhaps the young woman was playing a game with her. She knew the Inuits had vivid imaginations, and sometimes played games at night in the tent. If she wanted to play a game, she'd go along with her.

"And when does this magic canoe appear?" she asked.

"It must appear now, for the time has come," the young woman said.

"And where will it appear?" Jana asked.

"You must go to find it."

"And where shall I find it?" Jana asked, wondering how much longer she should go along with the game.

"It is hidden in the willows at the end of the lake. It is at the place where the loons lift into the air which tumbles from the land to the water."

Jana had watched the loons lift off the water several times. She wondered why they generally took off in one particular direction. Maybe this woman wasn't playing a game. She couldn't be sure. She'd play the game a bit longer, if that's what it took to find out.

"You will need the canoe to catch fish for Christine and yourself," the woman said.

"Have you decided to give up on fish?" Jana asked, half joking.

"I will leave in eight days," the woman said. "The summer seal hunt on the ice will be over. I will go back to help prepare the meat for winter. When the hunters come south to spear the caribou crossing the lake, they will take Christine home."

The young woman had not been playing a game. Jana felt a little ashamed she hadn't taken her seriously. It was the winter the young woman had on her mind; that was what was behind it all.

Winter! Just the sound of it sent a shiver up Jana's spine. What would she do if the injunction was not granted? Or what if it was slow in coming?

Ted had arranged with his Yellowknife Office to retain a lawyer to assist the lawyer she had retained. They would apply for a stop-work injunction, based on environmental concerns, the minute it was confirmed that Abscot Resources intended to involve Hansen Lake in their search for diamonds. It was assumed, that if the injunction was issued, Abscot Resources would press for an immediate trial.

Within three weeks of Jana's arrival at the lake, Ted

had received information confirming that Abscot Resources intended to tunnel under Hansen Lake. Shortly after, Jana received word that the stop-work injunction had been granted.

Abscot Resources had acted immediately, and been granted leave to challenge the injunction in court without delay. A trial date had been set for August 20. The venue would be Yellowknife.

Jana had been elated with word of the injunction. But she was not without worry about the trial. Ted said it would be a fight, and she had resolved to make it the fight of her life. Now she was afraid. What did she know of courts, and judges, and crown attorneys? They could make her look like a fool in five minutes, and her case would be lost. And with it would go Hansen Lake.

She needed someone to talk to. The younger woman would be gone the next day. Only the old lady would be left.

"I would like to speak to you," she said to the young woman, as she approached the door of the Inuit tent that evening. "It's a personal matter."

The young woman stopped putting clothing into her pack, and gave Jana her full attention. The old lady, catching the tone of Jana's voice, looked up from a half-finished moccasin and listened.

Jana told the two women about Glen being killed in the war, and about the lake being named for him.

"It's the only thing I have left that gives my life meaning," she said.

The young woman laid her hands on the children's shoulders.

"Our men leave us these," she said, "when they get killed in battles with polar bears, and walruses, and when they get lost in storms on the ice."

"Children?" the old lady questioned, looking straight at Jana.

"No," she answered.

"This lake...this Hansen Lake...this is your child?"

"Perhaps that is one way of expressing it," Jana replied.

"Then you must care for your child," the young woman said.

"Child," the old lady said, a slight smile squeezing the skin around her eyes. "Child," she repeated, and threaded the sinew through the hole in the soft caribou skin.

The sun was sliding obliquely toward the horizon as Jana wandered leisurely back to her tent.

When that sun rose again, she would rise with a fierce determination to protect the lake. That determination would have a kind of strength, missing when she walked into the Inuit tent earlier that evening, in the need to reach into the hearts of other women for direction.

When she told them why she had come to protect the lake, she watched for their reaction. It had seemed as though there was an immediate transfer of some of their strength to her. And she had a strange sense that that strength was meant to remain with her for the battle ahead.

Was it the emotion she showed when she went through the details of her relationship to the lake? Emotions to which she thought all women were naturally tuned? They didn't show much emotion.

There were some moments, in relating the details to the Inuit women, when the lake became as much a part of her as the blood coursing through her veins. Did the Inuit women sense that? Maybe they understood emotion, but didn't show it like other women did. Maybe their emotion was in the application of instinct, directed toward survival. Maybe in the harsh environment they could not afford to express it in any other way.

Was her own emotion an instinctive expression directed toward survival? Was that how the Inuit women saw it?

As she neared her tent, the thought struck her that in protecting the lake for herself, she might, in a sense, be protecting something for all women. The Inuit women might be looking at it that way.

Jana walked into the tent and closed the door for the night. As she began to undress, she tried to visualize the court room where the upcoming trial would take place.

She would be disciplined. Her defense of the lake would come from a clear head. She was certain about that. But she was also certain that defense would originate in her heart - a heart made stronger by the hearts of other women.

As she crawled into her sleeping bag, the call of a loon drifted across the lake and echoed faintly against the large rock. She listened for a while. She and the loon had something in common, she thought. They were both, in their own way, sending out a call in the Arctic night.

XXXI

Two R.C.M.P. officers were barring the door to a group of noisy environmentalists when Jana walked up the court house steps with her lawyer.

Inside, the court was packed with well-dressed men and women, a few natives, and a special summer school class of elementary school students accompanied by their teacher.

The lawyer led Jana to the front of the room and seated her near the large table reserved for counsellors. He opened his brief case, scanned the documents, and waited.

In a few minutes the door to the judge's chambers opened, and a black-robed, middle-aged man appeared. The crowd rose, and he walked directly to the bench. He spent a few minutes looking at the papers before him, then glanced down at the crown attorney and nodded.

"Your Honour," the Crown Attorney began, "this case concerns Hansen Lake in the District of Keewatin....

"A court injunction was issued against Abscot Resources after an investigation by the Department of The Environment for the Territories. Its purpose was to stop mining exploration work in the immediate area of Hansen Lake.

"The injunction prohibits further exploration work, until such time as Abscot Resources satisfies The Department of The Environment that any damage done to the environment will be within accept-

able limits. However, if the court should deem the
stop-work order to be unjust, and lift the injunction
in favour of Abscot Resources, the company will
have the legal right to continue the exploration
work, without interruption.

"The injunction was issued upon application by
a Madam Jana Hansen.

"There is a unique aspect to this case, brought
by Hansen, having to do with the naming of the lake
by the Canadian Permanent Committee on Geo-
graphical Names. The Department of The Environment has no jurisdiction in this area.

"There is one other issue which may enter into
the litigation, having to do with the assumed right,
by the Inuit people, to change the names of features
on certain lands. Here again, The Department of
The Environment has no jurisdiction.

"It follows, then, that while the Crown would
normally have the obligation to defend the injunction issued by The Department of The Environment, in the case of Abscot Resources versus
Hansen, the Crown believes it prudent to withdraw
from active participation in the trial, and assume
observer status, until such time as there may be
resolution of the problems presented by the unusual
aspects of the case, already referred to. At that time,

the Crown may, or may not wish to assume an active roll in the case.

"In conclusion, if I may, Your Honour, I wish to state: The Department of The Environment has not, heretofore, been required to deal with a case of such complexity, as the case now before the court.

"The Department awaits the decision of the court in the disposition of the case of Abscot Resources versus Hansen.

"Thank you, Your Honour."

The next words were blurred in the confusion scattering Jana's thoughts. The plan she and the lawyer worked out was nowhere to be found in her brain. She leaned ahead and whispered to him.

"What's happening? Where's Ted?"

"Sh!" the lawyer said. "Everything's all right. Just keep calm."

The judge turned his eyes to the attorneys for the plaintiff and defendant.

"Before we proceed with this case, I intend to provide an opportunity for the counsellors for the two parties (and I will include officials from The Department of Environment in any discussion) to determine if some agreement can be reached to preclude the necessity of litigation.

"This is a case in which a decision is to be

made, on whether or not continued exploration work by Abscot Resources will result in unacceptable environmental damage.

"There is another aspect to the case, concerning an individual whose husband was killed overseas, and in whose memory Hansen Lake is named. But the case hinges on whether or not there is just cause, in prohibiting further exploration work by Abscot Resources, in the immediate area of Hansen Lake.

"This case is unique, in that it is the first of its kind in the Territories, and I believe, the first of its kind in the nation. My ruling will set a precedent which will (barring an appeal court decision to the contrary) become the standard for such cases in the foreseeable future." He paused and looked down at the lawyers and Environmental officials.

"I'm prepared at this time, to provide the concerned parties the opportunity to consider the possibility of coming to a settlement, on the basis of serious discussion amongst yourselves."

When there was no movement on the part of either of the lawyers, or the Environmental officials, the judge pushed back his greying hair, nodded to the clerk, and brought the gavel down sharply.

"Call your first witness," he ordered.

Mr. Allen, the attorney for Abscot Resources,

jumped to his feet, and nodded to a well-dressed man of about fifty, who quickly stepped to the witness stand.

"State your name," the clerk ordered. The witness identified himself as Calvin Arntfield.

"Place your hand on the Bible. Do you swear to tell the truth and nothing but the truth?"

"I do," Mr. Arntfield stated. Mr. Allen turned to face his witness.

"Mr. Arntfield, you are an officer of the company known as Abscot Resources, are you not?"

"I am."

"Would you say your company has an admirable record when it comes to caring for the environment?"

"I believe that to be the case."

"In fact, your company has, in the past, carried out extensive studies on several of your mining properties before you began operations."

"Yes, that is true."

"Do you anticipate any serious damage to the lake in question, if you are allowed to proceed with your work?"

"No."

"And you have come to the conclusion that if

there was any damage it would be within an acceptable range."

"Yes."

"The Department of Environment has found no indication of damage to Hansen Lake thus far?"

"They have found no actual damage."

The attorney folded his arms and threw back his head. He stood for a moment, letting a broad smile spread across his countenance.

Did Mr. Arntfield have a substantial general knowledge of the mining industry? the attorney asked the witness. And an appreciation of the huge expenditure of funds required in prospecting and preliminary exploration? Did he also have particular knowledge of the kind of geological structures necessary for the containment of diamonds?

Mr. Arntfield smiled, and answered yes to all questions.

"And now you think you have the potential to create wealth, and provide substantial employment for working men, including the native population?" The lawyer moved up close to Mr. Arntfield, as though they might be having a personal conversation. The crowd strained their ears to catch Mr. Arntfield's answer.

"Yes," he said. "I don't think I would be exaggerating if I stated that this venture could result in immense benefit to the Territories in tax revenue and employment."

"Diamonds." The attorney paused. "That's what you're after."

"Yes."

"We all know the value of diamonds," the attorney stated. "In fact, you'd be looking for those diamonds this very minute if there was not an injunction preventing you from searching for the diamonds."

"That is correct."

"You are here for the purpose of getting the stop-work injunction lifted, so you can get back to looking for diamonds without delay."

"Yes."

"No more questions, Your Honour."

"Cross-examination," the judge called.

Mr. Smith glanced at Jana as he got up from the table. He walked slowly toward the witness stand, then raised his head sharply to face the witness.

"You have said your environmental record is admirable, have you not?"

"Yes, I believe so." Mr. Smith stared at him for several moments.

"Do you consider yourself to have a good memory, Mr. Arntfield?"

"I believe I do."

"Let me remind you of the case involving Wolf Island Mine. Was your company not charged with leaking cyanide into the lake?"

"Yes. There was some which escaped, unfortunately."

"And there was Red Mountain, was there not? Mercury, wasn't it?"

"It was another unfortunate accident."

"You were required to do a clean-up and pay substantial compensation. Is that right?"

"Yes. But let me advise you that we have had an unblemished record in the last seven years."

"You are aware, are you not, that there is a particular aspect in the case of Hansen Lake, having to do with how the lake got its name?"

"I have been informed that is the case. However, the injunction cites the physical environment of the area in question, and that is the only concern of our company."

"In your testimony you have painted an attractive picture, in which diamonds are almost within the hand. But the fact of the matter is your pronouncements are based mainly on speculation. Is that true?"

The witness hesitated. "It's not quite the way I would put it. We do have encouraging samples."

"It's still mainly speculation. Is that true?" Again the witness hesitated. The judge looked over, waiting for an answer to the question.

"Answer the question, Mr. Arntfield," he said.

"Yes."

"No more questions, Your Honour," Mr. Smith stated, and sat down.

The attorney for the company called the next witness, who was the company geologist. The questions were essentially the same as those already dealt with when Mr. Arntfield was on the stand. Mr. Smith felt no need to cross-examine.

It was now the right time to call Jana to the stand.

"State your name," the clerk ordered.

"Jana Hansen."

"Place your right hand on the Bible, and swear to tell the truth."

"I will not. I will not swear on the Bible," Jana stated firmly.

There was silence in the courtroom. The judge stared over at Jana.

"Madam, you must attest to the truth of your testimony. Our system of justice requires that you swear to do so. The Bible is traditional in this oath."

"I will not call on any God to witness the truth of my words."

The attorney for the mining company jumped to his feet.

"Your Honour, this witness is putting on a show to divert attention from the issue at hand."

The judge scowled at the attorney.

"Counsellor, do I have to remind you of court procedure? I will tolerate no further interruptions." He turned back to Jana. "Madam, I ask you to reconsider your statement."

"Your Honour, I cannot associate my testimony with the despicable passages contained in the Bible, and the horror stories of killing and other vile acts of those despicable characters who are presented as models for children."

"Madam, our courts still recognize the authority of the Bible in the solemn attestation to the truth of witnesses' words."

"Your Honour, if I were to quote passages from the Bible as my authority, would it be acceptable in this court of law?"

A thoughtful look came to the judge's face. He tapped his finger on his chin as he pondered her words.

"Madam, in this instance I will affirm you as a legitimate witness, if you promise to tell the truth."

Jana raised her right hand. "I promise to tell the truth," she said.

Jana's attorney, Mr. Smith, rose and asked Jana to state her full name.

"Hansen," he repeated, emphasizing the word. "The same name as the name denoting the lake."

"Yes."

"Would I be correct in assuming that you have been a widow for these many years since the death of your husband?"

"Yes."

"You have no children."

"No."

"Your husband was an airman?"

"Yes."

"A decorated airman?"

"Yes."

"His heroism helped to save their plane, severely damaged on a bombing run?"

"Yes."

"That is why he was decorated?"

"I believe that was the reason."

"And because of his act of heroism, a lake was named in his memory. Is that correct?"

"Yes."

"Hansen Lake?"

"Yes."

"It seems perfectly clear to me why you would want Hansen Lake preserved in its present, pristine state. But you think that lake may now be in danger?"

Mr. Allen jumped to his feet. "I object, Your Honour. What the witness thinks is irrelevant."

The judge thought for a moment, then stated, "What this witness thinks is, in this case, of primary importance. It is not a frivolous 'I think.' It is obvious that what the witness thinks is registered in deep concern for a lake. Objection overruled!"

"Your husband, along with thousands of other young men, and women, died to preserve freedom, and those other things which we, as a civilized and democratic society, hold dear. Would you agree with that statement?"

"Yes."

"This court room might well be symbolic of one of those things. Would you agree with that?"

"I would."

"No more questions, Your Honour."

An unusual calm settled over the courtroom. Two older men, wearing Canadian Legion blazers, kept nodding their heads and glancing at Jana.

Mr. Allen got slowly to his feet. He stared at Jana, then began to speak in a low, intimidating voice.

"Do you know what it means to be out of work, and subjected to a life of neglect and poverty?"

"I should," Jana replied. "I live on a reservation." The answer caught the lawyer by surprise, and he turned away for a moment.

"But you are not living in poverty."

"No."

"You are well looked after by our country."

"My answer to that requires qualification..."

"Just answer yes or no," the lawyer demanded. When she hesitated, the judge indicated that she must reply to the question.

"If you mean do I benefit from the freedom my husband fought for, the answer is yes. If you mean do I benefit directly in terms of support, the answer is no."

"You are a war widow, are you not?"

"I'm sure that has been well established," Jana replied.

"Our country supports war widows. Everyone knows that. It costs the country millions of dollars every year." He stared up at Jana. "One might assume that you receive a healthy pension in order to dress so elegantly."

"I do not accept one cent from our country in compensation for the loss of my husband," she said, her voice rising. "No amount of money could ever buy his blood." She felt herself losing the discipline she had determined to maintain.

"But our country does use you well. You admitted that," the lawyer stated. "It is not as though this country deprives you of anything. The fact is, in your petition, you are attempting to deprive this country of the opportunity to provide a good life for some of its people, for its children! And for the children who come after them..." The lawyer looked straight at her.

"Think about the lives of the children," he said, then added, "I understand you have no children to worry about."

"You know I haven't!" she shouted. "This country took from me the only thing that made life worthwhile."

"Try to control yourself, madam," the judge called. But it was too late for control. It was too late now for anything but an explosive release of emotion.

"This country robbed my husband of his final

leave," she cried. "I would have been fertile at that time. We had waited. This country robbed me of the only chance I had to conceive his child. Does this court understand that? Does anybody understand that?" She slumped down in the witness chair, sobbing into her scarf.

Some of the middle-aged wives of the mining executives held handkerchiefs to their eyes, while their husbands looked straight ahead.

"This court will stand adjourned until ten o'clock tomorrow morning," the judge declared.

As Mr. Smith led Jana from the courtroom, several of the wives glanced in her direction with understanding expressions.

Two little Inuit girls, too young for the outburst of emotion, cried loudly. Their teacher comforted them, then hustled the class out the back door a security guard held open for them.

"I'm not sure where we're at, this far into the trial," Mr. Smith said, when Jana seemed settled. "Something's got to happen one way or another to sway that judge. At the moment, I'd say we'd better stick to the strategy we've worked out. That will require that we both exercise the utmost discipline. I'm counting heavily on you in that respect."

Jana nodded her head.

After a quiet supper, Jana read for a while, then

prepared for bed. On this night she would use one of the sleeping pills she'd brought. Tomorrow it would be over.

The lake was not yet lost. If there was a chance of saving it, she'd be ready. She turned on the bedside radio and slipped into bed.

The news was an extended version, reporting a great deal of detail about the trial. Perhaps there was more interest in the case than she had imagined.

She thought of the lake, sitting serene in the tundra. Christine would be in her tent working the caribou skins into winter clothing. By her side would be a loaded rifle, and outside would be a dog, its belly satisfied with fresh fish.

She had begun to realize how much the lake meant to the old lady. "Many seasons of the caribou," Christine said. Jana hoped when she returned she'd be able to tell her the lake was safe.

At ten o'clock sharp, Judge Brandon came through the doors of his chambers and walked quickly to the bench. He scanned the documents before him.

"The case of Abscot Resources versus Hansen. Call your first witness, Mr. Allen." He smoothed his hair back with his right hand, then pushed himself back in his chair.

The attorney for Abscot Resources called Mr. Arntfield to the stand. The witness reiterated what he had stated previously, about benefits which would accrue to the people if exploration was allowed to continue. Jana's lawyer, Mr. Smith, did not cross-examine the witness.

The next witness called was an Inuit man who was sitting with the mining executives. His Inuit name was Ummilik, he said, but his English name was David Charles.

"You are a member of The Land Claims Council, are you not?"

"Yes."

"In connection with land claims, your council sometimes petitions the government to change the names of settlements?"

"Yes."

"Might a name change apply to a section of land?"

"Yes."

The lawyer unfolded a topographic map and showed it to the witness, then handed it up to the bench. "This complete section carries the name of a prominent feature on the map. In this case, the section and the feature carry the name Hansen Lake."

"Yes."

"Is it in your plan to request a name change for Hansen Lake?"

"It will be considered," David Charles replied.

There was a shuffling at the back of the room. One of the men wearing a Legion blazer was obviously upset. He attempted to rise, while another Legion member tried to restrain him. The judge called for order, and quiet was restored to the courtroom.

Jana's lawyer did not cross-examine the witness. He did not think the public would stand for erasing names of decorated service men from history.

The lawyer for Abscot Resources called Jana Hansen to the stand.

"You have heard what Mr. Charles said about reclaiming his land, and applying Inuit names to its features, have you not?"

"I have," Jana acknowledged.

"If a name change came about for Hansen Lake, you would have no legitimate claim to it. What do you think of that?"

"I object!" Mr. Smith shouted, jumping to his feet. "What my client thinks is not the business of the counsellor nor of this court."

"Objection sustained."

"Let me put it this way," Mr. Allen said, staring up at Jana. "You are presenting yourself as one who has a degree of sovereignty over this lake, when in fact you have no right to any part of it. Is that not true?"

"You are quite wrong in your accusation. I have never claimed any part of the lake."

"Yet you stand in the way of those who would exercise their right to ownership of the lake."

Discipline, Jana reminded herself. Discipline. But it was of no use. The blood rushed into her neck and burned up into her face.

The lawyer stood before her, his eyes accusing.

"All you have is a name on a piece of paper," he said. "Hansen Lake. What does it amount to? Two simple words, that's all. And when the name is changed you'll have nothing!"

Jana started to reply, but any logical argument she might have presented was lost. She jumped to her feet.

"Take it!" she cried, "Take the lake! The country has taken everything else in life that mattered. Now take the lake! Take it! Take it!" She collapsed into the chair.

A noisy disturbance at the door prompted the judge to call for order, but the noise grew louder.

"You can't come in," a court officer shouted, as an old Inuit woman tried to force her way into the courtroom.

"Let her in," some spectators demanded and offered to give up their seats. Finally, the officer relented and let the woman in. She walked straight to the bench carrying a rolled-up bundle of caribou skins, and stood staring at the judge.

"Who is this woman?" he demanded.

"What is your name?" the court clerk asked.

"Christine."

"Why is she here?" the judge asked.

"For this woman," Christine answered, pointing to Jana.

"What is your submission?" the judge demanded. The old lady was confused.

"See what this woman is about," he ordered, looking over to the clerk.

"Have you something to say?" the court clerk asked politely.

"This woman...the lake," Christine said. "I come for her."

She unrolled several layers of caribou skin and removed an age-bleached scroll. It appeared to be about twelve inches, both in length and width. Around the edges were many small caricatures of animals, and in the centre was an inscription.

"Where did you get this?" the judge asked the old lady.

"Mother, many mothers," Christine replied. She began explaining about the scroll in the Inuit language.

"Is there anyone in the courtroom who might wish to interpret what this woman is saying?" the judge asked.

There was some excitement in the elementary school class, as two young Inuit girls started whispering loudly to each other.

"Rosie," the teacher called, "You and Ella speak the Inuit language. Would you like to tell the judge what the lady is saying?" The two girls smiled and nodded their assent. The teacher took them over to the bench and had them stand by the old lady.

After a lengthy conversation with Christine, they were ready to translate what she related to them.

They told the judge about the white man who came with Indians from the south. The Indians went wild when they saw an Eskimo camp. They came in the dark and killed all the people. People from another camp found them in the morning.

When that white man came back from the

northern sea to the lake, he and his Indians were starving, and the Eskimo people fed them and saved their lives. One woman at the lake was this lady's great-great-grandmother.

The white man wrote something on the caribou skin, and told them to keep it forever, to show the lake and land would be protected by a great king who lived far away in another land.

The judge handed the scroll to the court clerk and asked him to try to read what was written. It was not legible to the naked eye, with the exception of two words at the bottom. A magnifying glass was brought from the judge's chamber, and the clerk proceeded to read.

"In grateful acknowledgement to the people of this broad land, I hereby declare in the name of His Royal Highness George III, Sovereign of the British Realm, that this land shall ever be the preserve of the people whose heritage is this land. Let it be said that this virgin land was here when the white man came, and it shall be here when the history of the white man is but a whisper upon the winds of destiny. Samuel Hearne 1771." The clerk paused, then stated that there were two more words and a date which read: Bravo! Nicholson 1958.

The judge sat pondering the words for some

time, then asked if the counsellors wished to present any further argument. When both attorneys declined, he declared the court adjourned until ten o'clock the next morning, at which time he would render his decision.

Jana hurried to Christine. "How did you get here?" she demanded.

"In the yellow plane."

"Mark?"

"Yes."

Christine told Jana about Mark dropping off two young geologists at a mining exploration site a few miles from Hansen Lake. On his return he ran into a fierce headwind. He stopped to empty the extra gas into the planes's tanks, and to wait for the wind to die down. Christine gave him tea, and they sat in the tent talking about the caribou crossing the lake in the spring and fall.

Mark said he wondered how the first white explorer felt when he came upon the lake. That's when she remembered the scroll. She told Mark that she would go with him to the place where Jana was fighting to save the lake which was named for her young husband.

Mr. Smith walked over to where Jana and Christine were sitting. He smiled at Christine.

"I'll arrange a place for her at the Sally Ann," he told Jana. "They know how to look after ladies like her."

Judge Brandon sat down and placed his large hands firmly on the arms of his chair. He looked out at the packed courtroom, his face sober and calm.

"I have deliberated at length on the submissions to the court by the witnesses and their counsellors, and on the exhibit, which in the late hours of the session was brought to the bench.

"It is unusual when exhibits, of which the justice has no former knowledge, are allowed as evidence. Because of the particular circumstances surrounding the case of Abscot Resources versus Hansen, I allowed the presentation of the exhibit." The judge leaned back in his chair and paused for a few seconds.

"When this case began, I stated that it was a case which had no precedent in Canadian Law. There was nothing in case records to be consulted as a guide in proceeding toward a decision which would be fair to the parties involved. The conclusion I have come to is based on my judgement of what is just and reasonable."

Several of the spectators sat on the edge of their seats, waiting nervously for the decision, but it was not to come immediately, as they had expected, and the judge continued to address the court. They sat back, waiting for a signal that a decision would be imminent.

"Because Abscot Resources have, in the past, been responsible for environmental damage, we cannot assume that Abscot Resources would take a careless attitude about the environment, in the case of Hansen Lake. We have no proof that such would be the case.

"It would be a wrongful decision to come to, if that decision was made on the basis of an assumption of future environmental damage.

"In the case before us, there is another factor which must be taken into consideration. That is the naming of the lake.

"It is facts we derive from witnesses' testimony that we must subject to reason, and sometimes those facts are charged with emotion. We cannot allow ourselves to be swayed by emotion. However, there are instances when profound thoughts of human beings have, in their pronouncements, an emotional appeal. In such instances the pronouncements need not be dismissed outright.

"In the case before us, the scroll reminds us of the temporal nature of man's existence. Implicit in the words on the scroll is the profound message that we must preserve the land and its people.

"The lake in question is, in this instance, a special part of the land. It carries the name of a young man who died in the preservation of justice.

"If we lose sight of the sacrifice of thousands of young men and women, in the name of freedom, we will be in danger of sacrificing the principles which permit us to call ourselves a civilized society, and our nation a civilized nation.

"The land means the land mass, as well as everything on it and under its surface. It includes the water, the birds and the animals. And it includes the minerals which we must have to maintain our modern society. That is a fact - a fact we cannot ignore. However, in dealing with such facts, we cannot allow ourselves to forget values, if we are to maintain our civilized society.

"There are situations in which values must take precedence over all else. This is one of those situations. In the case of Abscot Resources versus Hansen, my decision comes down on the side of Hansen."

Loud cheers and applause greeted the judge's decision. Some of the women accompanying the mining executives applauded, while their husbands sat in stunned silence.

Two reporters made their way toward Jana, as others tried to batter their way through the crowd jamming the doors.

"Who would have thought the old lady had such guts?" one reporter said, as he came close to Jana. "She's the one who tipped the scales. No doubt about that."

"Who was the Nicholson on the scroll?" the other reporter wondered, as they approached Jana.

Jana had little to say except that she was pleased. Yes, she would be going back to the lake with Christine, she told the reporters, as Mr. Smith guided Christine over to sit with her. Probably until near freeze-up, she said, in answer to the next question.

"Did your brother-in-law have some reason for staying away from the trial?" a reporter asked.

"I know of none."

"It's strange he wouldn't want to protect a lake named for his brother."

"You are wrong," Jana replied emphatically. "There is some legitimate reason for his absence."

"Perhaps," the reporter said, and walked quickly toward the door. He turned back and asked, "Where is the old lady staying tonight?" Mr. Smith shook his head in a 'no comment' gesture, and the reporter left.

Jana went to her hotel room after having supper with Mr. Smith. She realized how exhausted she was when she could barely lift her heavy briefcase to the closet shelf. She would go to bed without delay.

Mark would be there early in the morning to return her and Christine to the lake. There would be much for her and Christine to do while the warm days lasted.

She turned on the radio and began to undress. It was good to listen to music again, after the noise and the stress of the last three days.

"Here is the ten o'clock news:

"A geologist and his student assistant have been rescued by a helicopter in a remote section of the Yukon. The two men had been missing for three days. The geologist told the reporter it came about because he lost his glasses. His shortsightedness, and the assistant's unfamiliarity with the terrain, prevented them from finding their way back to the base camp. The geologist, Ted Hansen, said he would never go into the bush again without two pairs of glasses."

Jana turned off the radio and sat down on the bed. She let herself fall gently over onto the soft pillow. It had been a momentous day.

XXXII

The canoe glided effortlessly across the pastel blue surface of the lake. Christine sat in the bow, directing Jana to an area on the far shore where the eider ducks nested.

"The eggs are good," she said, "unless a woman has a baby in her belly. Then the eggs make her sick." As they neared the shore, a fox scurried into a patch of dwarf willows at the top of the bank.

"It looks as though we may be too late," Jana remarked.

"Even a fox can't find all the nests," Christine replied.

Christine was already tasting those strong eggs, Jana thought. She had talked about them for several days. She said they'd be a nice change after the fish. Soon they would be too far hatched. If they were more than half hatched she didn't cook them. There'd be some fresh ones for Jana, she said.

They pulled the canoe up on shore and started searching along the edge of the water for the nests. In a frantic flutter of wings, a duck shot past them within a few inches of their heads.

"Angry," Christine said. The duck circled and came back accompanied by another duck. They swooped low over their heads, spraying foul-smelling excrement which just missed Jana.

"Angry," Christine repeated. When they reached the nest they found five eggs, some of which were covered with excrement.

"They're still good," Christine said. "We'll leave two. Maybe there's another nest."

They found three nests, all empty. The fox had cleaned out the eggs. Jana felt ashamed that they had robbed the first nest of three eggs, but Christine was not concerned. There were lots of ducks this year, she said. In a bad year they wouldn't take the eggs unless they needed them for food.

As Christine led Jana through the spongy muskeg, she stopped abruptly. She stepped back and slowly lifted her arm, pointing to a spot in front of her. It took some time for Jana to distinguish between the duck and the surrounding vegetation.

"She thinks we don't see her," Christine said.

"I hope she'll fool the fox like she fooled me," Jana remarked.

Jana and Christine spent many days in the canoe. They explored every bay and inlet, and walked over the pollywog-shaped island at the end of the lake. They fished sometimes, and they landed the canoe to take closer looks at the burrows in the banks, where the wolves had reared their young in safety, and where the wolverines had preyed on lemmings and arctic hares.

They discovered particular areas where the spongy muskeg sprang back up in rhythm with their steps. Sometimes they stood bouncing the ground just to feel it respond, and watching the undulating waves spread out over its surface. And they rested occasionally where a profusion of flowers lent colour to the eye, and fragrance, in intoxicating generosity, to the nose.

The days spent in the canoe and exploring the shores were happy days. Jana knew she would absorb enough in sight, sound and smell to last for the rest of her life, for she would never return to the lake. The memories she took with her now would take their place with the others she had safely stored so long ago.

Christine often told Jana stories about the migrating caribou, and how they speared them from kayaks when they swam across the lake. They asked their spirits for forgiveness. Taking their lives meant meat and clothing for winter, she said. Frozen, raw caribou was delicious. Sometimes they would kill a stray caribou in winter, but the meat was not delicious because it was without fat.

When the snow started to melt, there would be reindeer moss for the caribou to eat. Then they would begin their migration to the calving grounds by the northern sea. The pregnant females would come first with the young, and the wolves would be in close pursuit. Two weeks later the males would follow the females. "It was a glorious sight which made our hearts ready for spring," Christine said.

One evening, Christine told Jana how her father was killed by a polar bear. He was sliding along on his belly toward a seal sunning itself by its hole in the ice. When the seal slept for a few seconds, her father would move closer. A polar bear was hiding behind the ice hummocks, and moving toward the seal also, but none of the hunters saw him. When her father was very close to the seal, the polar bear jumped over a hummock and killed the seal with one swipe of its sharp claws. Then the bear came after her father so he wouldn't get the seal. Her father got up to fight the bear, but he was cold from the ice and he was too slow. Her family was watching from a distance, and two hunters went and killed the bear.

Christine was quiet for some time.

"Many men were killed by bears, walruses and blizzards," she said.

That evening, when Jana left Christine's tent to walk back to her own tent, the northern lights were dancing wildly across the sky in deep green, orange, violet and purple. Near the end of the display, the sky became blood red. And then...it was over. The star-filled sky shone in silvery brilliance for a couple of hours, then dissolved in a lake of fluid orange washing up from below the horizon. Soon the pale, yellow sun peeked above the horizon. It staggered sideways until it was whole, then rose to wander obliquely toward the heavens, and the beginning of a new day.

The next morning Jana noticed Christine looking up at the large rock sheltering the alpine roses. After some time she asked her what she was looking at.

"It's where I will lie at the end of the last season of the caribou," she replied. "It is where I was born, and many mothers before me."

"Christine, let's not talk of such things. Let's go for a swim and wash those things away. The days are getting shorter, and it will soon be too cold to swim."

But the old lady would not go swimming. She

would walk into the water along the shore and wash herself.

They began rebuilding the sod house, making a little more progress each day, as their skills improved. It would be a safe shelter if the weather turned suddenly cold.

"It will be warm in the sod house," Christine said. "We must wear jewellery when we bare our breasts, so we will look more like ladies." Jana just smiled, and resisted any remark which might embarrass the old lady.

As they worked on the house one cool day, Jana began telling Christine about the Indian summer, which came before winter, back where she lived. Christine had difficulty in understanding the meaning of the term.

"Two summers?" she asked.

"No, it's not really summer, but it's warm like summer. It comes late in the season, sometimes after we have had a touch of winter."

Christine shook her head in disbelief.

"It's beautiful," Jana told her, "and the colours of the trees are spectacular."

None of it made any sense to Christine. Still,

she seemed intrigued by the thought of a place where such a strange thing could happen.

"You should come home with me and see it," Jana suggested one day.

"No," the old lady said. "I would miss the caribou. Frozen caribou is delicious with tea."

"Love is delicious with or without tea," Jana remarked, in a whimsical mood.

"Love?" the old lady asked. What was the love this woman talked about? She never understood what it meant.

"Like the taste of frozen caribou?" she asked.

"Oh, I was just being silly," Jana said.

That evening Christine invited Jana for tea. She wanted to know more about the love Jana talked about, when she spoke of her young husband.

"Why did you want this thing you call love?" Christine asked.

"In our culture, it's something every girl desires when she reaches a certain age...when she is becoming a woman."

"When she can have babies?"

"Yes...I think it would be correct to put it that way."

"How did it happen with your man?"

"It was physical attraction at first. Then something inside me made me want to be close to him. After a while I wanted him to kiss me and hold me tightly in his arms. My feelings of affection for him became so intense, I wanted our two bodies to become one."

"We put our bodies together because we needed what we got from the man's body," Christine said. "Is that it?"

"It's part of it. That comes about through intense desire for the person, because you love him."

"Sometimes our women got babies they didn't need," Christine said.

"I didn't."

"Didn't you feel the need to put your body together with another man, sometimes?"

Jana hesitated. "Yes," she finally answered.

"Did you find another man?"

Again Jana hesitated. Should she tell Christine about the affairs? Would she understand?

"A healthy young woman needs a man," Christine said.

Jana told Christine about the young engineer Ted had introduced her to, and that she left him because of his heavy drinking.

"Later, I joined an arts club in the city, mostly

for the weekend dances. I was involved with two men while I was a member of the club. Each time I thought I was falling in love again."

"This love must be a very strange thing," Christine said, shaking her head.

"I finally realized that it was always simply physical love. I knew I would never find the love I once had with Glen. And I knew I could never have a child by any other man."

"The lake is your child," Christine said. "Your husband gave you that child."

Jana smiled. She thought back to the day she and Glen lay together and decided when she would try to conceive his child.

She never conceived that child.

The old lady watched her, as she sat with twitching legs, seeming not to want to leave the strange world she was remembering.

After a few moments, Jana got up and folded her arms across her chest. Christine's eyes followed her, reading her face.

"Are you thinking of Indian summer?" she asked.

"Indian summer is like love," Jana said, "warm, mellow, sweet with pungent fragrance.

"Love is...love is like a butterfly, soft and gentle..." It wasn't always soft and gentle. Sometimes it was rough and desperate, almost cruel. But in springtime, when the world was waking to the fragrance of blossoms, and the sweetness of bird songs, love was soft and gentle.

"Spring..." Jana stopped abruptly. That second year...so long ago. She was in the garden by the path that led down to the spring. Glen drank deeply of the cold water she brought. Fresh, cold water was the next best thing to love, he said. They had tasted both that morning.

Christine was looking at her, waiting for the next words.

"Spring?" she questioned.

"It's like love in waltz time," Jana remarked.

"Love in waltz time? Waltz?"

"Here, I'll show you," Jana said, leading Christine out of the tent into the approaching twilight. She looked for a flat spot, then slowly began to waltz, counting "one, two, three...one, two, three..." She had only turned a few times, when her excited heart began to rush the blood into her breasts, and up to her face, burning into her ears and eyes. She forgot Christine.

At that moment she was the only woman on earth. She was a student of nature. She was the master of nature. She floated; she flew; she spun crazily; spilling her emotion into the cool air, as she spilled hot urine down her thighs. It did not matter. She was the only woman in the world. She had found a spirit which claimed a woman's strength as its sister.

"Jana!" Christine called out in alarm. "What makes you act so crazy?" The old lady's face showed deep concern, the way it did when she told of her mother taking off all her clothes and walking into the cold lake to perish.

Jana searched for a way to explain her emotions, but could find no words, while her breasts continued to throb in painful happiness.

"Love in waltz time." Christine shook her head in bewilderment. "Crazy!"

"Let's go into the lake," Jana suggested. "Let's wash off all our concerns and wild emotions."

A suspicious look flashed in Christine's eyes, as if she thought this Jana was crazy, after all.

"I'll build the flames for our tea," she said, quickly going to the tent.

Jana removed her clothes and walked toward the lake. The stars were starting to appear in the clear, quiet sky. It was a night like the one she visualized when her ballet teacher talked about *The*

Barcarole. O lovely night...O night of love...Time flies and carries away our caresses...carries them away forever....

The happy days at the lake were coming to an end. In a couple of weeks the north wind would lay threads of silver lace on the surface of the lake, telling of the winter that was on its way. The weakening sun would become a dim ghost on the distant horizon. The stragglers, following the migrating caribou, would send a chorus of tinkling crystal ringing down the lake, as their anxious hoofs crashed their way through the thickening blue ice.

Jana wished she could persuade Christine to go home with her, but Christine seemed determined to stay at the lake, with only the dog and rifles as her companions. She would go back with the hunters, when they came to spear the caribou, in their fall migration. It would only be a few days now, she said.

There was one week to go before the engine of Mark's plane would break the silence of early morning. The plane would swoop in low over the lake and soar a few feet above the water, then let down, sending spray flying as the pontoons struck the water. Jana would slip on her parka, and walk down to the shore with two small suitcases. She would hand them to Mark, then step up onto a pontoon and climb into the plane. Mark would push the throttle, and the engine's roar would echo down the lake. The Cessna would gather speed and rise up on its pontoons, then lift into the air. She would ask Mark to circle around the lake once, to confirm the accuracy of her memory's recording. Then he would set the compass for Yellowknife.

On the evening of the last day, Jana rechecked her belongings, and placed them by the door. She'd be ready the moment the yellow float plane came into view.

She was reluctant to visit Christine's tent, for she worried she might not be able to control her emotions, and she did not want to upset the old lady. Christine had suggested it might be her last season of the caribou, and that bothered her.

Jana looked out of her tent that evening, deliberating on whether or not she should visit Christine. As she watched, Christine came out of her tent and walked toward her. When she was near enough she called, "Come, I have tea. We can talk once more." Jana turned from her tent and stepped quickly to join Christine.

They sat with cups of hot tea and some leftover

cookies. Jana listened as Christine told of the white fathers pouring water on their heads, and calling them christians. The fathers made them abide by the church laws. The lake was her church, she said. It was a church where there were no walls; where their hearts could chase the rolling clouds; where the spirits of human children could gather with the spirits of all the children of creation. Her spirit would come back to rest there after the last season of the caribou.

The white man, Nicholson, was a good man, she said. He came to the lake one time, after the white man's war, when the big eagles flew over the land to make maps. He said the maps would help the people to mark the paths of the caribou.

The white man, Nicholson, watched with her one night when a young buck caribou stood on a ridge in the moonlight, crying like a baby for a mate.

When she told him about the first white man writing something on caribou skin, he was very excited, and asked to see it. When he read it with his thick glass, he said it was very important. That's why she took it to the judge, she said.

Christine said an elder told her, in his life, every morning was the beginning of something new, and every evening ended with the glow of the next day's dawn. That's the way her life had been, she said. That's the way life should be, she thought.

Jana walked back to her tent in the deepening twilight. She had been rewarded once again. After tomorrow, the rewards would be only in the form of memories.

It was not yet daylight when Christine tapped on the door of Jana's tent.

"The dog is dead!" she called.

"What is it? What's wrong?"

"The dog is dead," Christine repeated.

"What happened?" Jana demanded. "What happened?"

"It was the big can," Christine said. "It was leaking and the dog licked it."

It was the drum of antifreeze belonging to the mining company, Jana realized. Bob offered to leave it to make room for a crate of rocks she gathered for a small cenotaph at the school. The drum had fallen off the ledge when they tried to move it to hide the paddles. Neither of them thought to look for leaks. It didn't take much antifreeze to kill a dog.

"Now a bear might come," Christine stated.

"And you alone here for two weeks before the hunters arrive? We're not going to have that. We'll work out something while we're burying the dog."

Christine had placed a can of water near the dog's mouth.

"What's that for?" Jana inquired.

"It is for the dog's spirit if it is thirsty."

"But it can't drink it." Jana protested.

"No, but it will know I have offered it, and that I ask forgiveness for my carelessness."

As they shovelled the last of the dirt into the hole where the dog lay on the permafrost, Christine eyed Jana with a questioning look. Jana thought she might be thinking of going with her, but she promised not to ask her again. After a minute's silence, when neither of them said a word, Christine switched her gaze to her tent, then quickly back to Jana.

"Will it be Indian summer?" she asked.

"Yes," Jana replied. "It will be Indian summer." Christine smiled, and reached out for Jana's hand.

They hurried to gather Christine's clothes, her needles, and a roll of caribou skins. They would be ready when Mark's plane arrived.

XXXIII

Jana looked up at the clock. Four hours had passed since she called Bob Conlon at Arcticair. Her cold coffee cup, still half full, sat on the desk by the telephone. She emptied it in the sink, and turned to the cupboard. She started to reach for the coffee, then stopped before her fingers touched the jar. This time it would be tea.

She waited until she thought the tea would be well brewed, the way Christine would have liked it. She removed the lid of the teapot and sniffed its bouquet, then poured a cup, and walked to the window.

All but a few scattered patches of the previous night's snow had disappeared under the attack of a more determined sun. It seemed that spring had leapt ahead in the four hours since she last looked over to the woodlot.

If only Christine could have seen the coming of spring! Instead, she would lie in her final resting place by the lake, where she had seen so many migrations of the caribou, in spring and fall.

The female caribou, accompanied by the young, would have started their long migration to the calving grounds by the northern sea. There would be tens of thousands, if they had wintered well in the fringe area of the boreal forest. They would be approaching the lake before long, with the wolves in close pursuit, culling out the weaker ones.

The male caribou came by two or three weeks later, Christine said.

Jana looked over to the slender saplings at the edge of the woodlot, where she saw a deer in the early morning. It was easy to trick herself into thinking it was a caribou. But the reality was that she would never again see caribou in the wild.

She moved the seven photographs from her desk to the shelf above the record player, where they looked out across the field to the woodlot. She let her eyes rest for a moment on each of the photographs, beginning with her mother's.

Those beautiful, blue eyes had lost direction in their search for reality, much too early in life. Finally, there was no reality.

Her father's kind eyes had found a path to progress, without losing sight of their cultural heritage. Polio had struck the light from those eyes when her father was in the prime of life.

Enoch's clear eyes had discovered a reality of their own in his lifetime. At the end, his spirit slipped away to join the spirits of the other children of creation.

Christine's dim eyes flashed in surprise when they fell upon the fiery, red maples of Indian summer. "Blood?" she questioned. "Oh, no, there's no blood..." Her answer stopped short when she remembered that first time, just in from the edge of the forest.

Laura Hansen's eyes were tied to a world of hard labour. They looked up some days to see, in the distance, a world where all children would be educated and healthy, where they had a chance to develop free from indoctrination and superstition.

Jimmy, whose eyes saw a world in which he would "amount to something," followed those eyes, until they saw nothing but blackness.

And Glen, whose young eyes looked out to a world of love; a world filled with adventure; a world in which every beat of his heart would celebrate the glory of being alive.

Jana stood back and looked again at the seven photographs. Memories. That's all she had left. That's all any of us has left, she thought. For what else is there in the end?

She walked to the kitchen window and looked down the lane to the lilac tree. The children would soon be there to walk her to their ballet class in the community centre. The two white girls, from across the river, told her they might bring a young neighbourhood child with them the next time they came.

The children were not memories. They were real.

At two o'clock she saw them coming into view. She closed the kitchen door, and started down the lane to meet them. When she was halfway to the lilac tree they called out to her.

"Good afternoon Miss 'P'."

Jana laughed when she thought of the day she did a pirouette, and in a whimsy said, "I'm Miss Pirouette!" Some of the small children could not pronounce pirouette, and settled for Miss 'P'. It became an endearing term all the children adopted.

As she drew closer, the children brought a small girl to the front of the group. They unbuttoned the child's coat and slipped it off, revealing a ballet costume with white stockings.

Her black hair was neatly swept back, revealing a high forehead. She had a rather striking profile for a child, Jana thought. She stepped quickly to the small girl and picked her up. She pressed her to her bosom for a moment, then put her down when she saw the surprised faces of the other children.

"Her name is Alicia Summers," one of the white girls stated. "We call her 'Indian Summers' because she is a little bit Indian."

The children laughed.

"She already knows some things about ballet," they chorused. "We taught her!"

"Well, shall we see if she's ready for a recital?" Jana asked.

The three-year old girl's brown eyes flashed in anticipation.

"Alicia?" Jana called. The child took two steps forward and did a quick curtsey. She pulled her small form erect, and reached out her slim fingers for Jana's hand.

"Good Afternoon," she said.